'Which roc

'Seven-thirtee

Louise gasped in surprise. 'Why, that's next door to me.'

His eyes opened slowly, something glittering in their depths that chilled her to the bone. 'I know.'

How could he manage to make a simple statement sound like an accusation? And why should he want to?

Jennifer Taylor was born in Liverpool, England, and still lives in the north-west, several miles outside the city. Books have always been a passion of hers, so it seemed natural to choose a career in librarianship, a wise decision as the library is where she met her husband, Bill. Twenty years and two children later, they are still happily married, with the added bonus that she has discovered how challenging and enjoyable writing romantic fiction can be!

Recent titles by the same author:

LOVESTORM
JUNGLE FEVER
DESERT MOON
TIDES OF LOVE

PLAYING AT LOVE

BY

JENNIFER TAYLOR

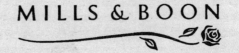

MILLS & BOON

MILLS & BOON and the Rose Device
are trademarks of the publisher.
Harlequin Mills & Boon Limited,
Eton House, 18-24 Paradise Road, Richmond, Surrey, TW9 1SR
This edition published by arrangement with Harlequin Enterprises B.V.

© Jennifer Taylor 1994

ISBN 0 263 78461 4

Set in Times Roman 11 on 12 pt
01-9510-51291 C

Made and printed in Great Britain

CHAPTER ONE

SHE'D noticed the man before, several times if she was honest. Only that morning she'd passed him on the terrace and smiled a greeting, but he'd cut her dead. His pale blue eyes had been cold as ice as they'd skimmed her face before he'd slipped on the mirrored sunglasses he habitually wore. Mortified by such a deliberate slight, Louise had hurried on her way, silently promising never to put herself in the position whereby he could do the same again, but as her gaze shifted back to him now it seemed she just might have to break that promise.

Despite the deep tan, his face was pale, his mouth beneath the heavy black moustache drawn into a thin line of white, beads of perspiration gleaming on his forehead. It was obvious to her practised eyes that he was in some kind of discomfort and, while she didn't relish the thought of inviting another put-down, she couldn't sit there and ignore the fact that he might be ill.

Reluctantly she got up and glanced round the hotel's deserted foyer, wishing that Carol were there to lend her support, but her friend had left over half an hour before to meet Simon and spend the evening at one of Miami's hot spots. There was only her left to offer help, it seemed.

'Are you all right?' She bent over the tall figure slumped in the chair, jumping nervously as his eyes opened and he glared up at her.

'Does it look as though I am?' he snarled through pain-stiffened lips. 'I should have thought it was obvious how I feel. Now if you don't mind, I don't feel like making small talk right now.'

Louise took a deep breath, forcing herself to stand her ground when what she really felt like doing was turning tail and running from such open hostility. Pain did odd things to a person, as she knew only too well from her nursing experience. She would give him the benefit of the doubt . . . just once.

'Would you like me to call someone—a doctor, perhaps?'

'No! What I want is for you to leave me alone. Understand? Aghhh!' He doubled over, his face going ashen, his eyes closing as a sudden violent spasm hit him, and Louise decided there and then that enough was enough. Sometimes one had to act against a person's wishes for his own good.

Briskly she slipped a hand under his elbow, her voice cool yet commanding as she waited for the attack to pass then started to urge him to his feet. 'I understand that you are ill, and, frankly, that's all I need to understand. Just tell me which room you're in and I'll help you back there; then we can decide if you need a doctor or not.'

'We? When did this become a joint decision? Who asked you to poke your nose in where it's not wanted, Miss . . . ?' He paused, although whether out of a desire to learn her name, which she rather doubted, or because a fresh bout of pain almost bent him double again, Louise had no real way of knowing. However, rather than labour the point with him in such a state, she volunteered the information anyway.

'Carter. Louise Carter. Now do you think you can stand by yourself or shall I see if I can find a porter to help?'

He cursed volubly, perspiration trickling down his face to catch in the thick hair on his upper lip. 'I don't need a porter! I don't need anyone. And I especially don't need you here playing the Good Samaritan, if indeed that's the role you're playing now!'

There was just something about the way he said that, just the tiniest inflexion in his deep voice, that made Louise wonder exactly what he meant, before she pushed it to the back of her mind. He might not need her help, but by heavens he was going to get it. He'd annoyed her just enough to make certain of that!

She took her hand away from his arm, smiling sweetly as she watched him sink heavily back down on to the chair. 'Please yourself, of course. If you would rather stay here, then obviously that's up to you.' She ran a hand over her short dark curls, her grey eyes reflecting a hint of distaste as she glanced around the lobby then let them drift back to his face. 'I would hate the idea of being ill in such a public place as this, but if it doesn't bother you then that's fine.' She shrugged lightly, then turned to pick up her bag from the table and head towards the lifts.

'Wait a minute!'

There was a rasp of authority in the deep voice now that turned what might have been intended as a request into an order, and Louise took immediate and unreasonable exception to it. Her spine stiffened imperceptibly and she carried on walking, the heels of her cream leather sandals clicking angrily on the marble floor.

'Miss . . . Carter, wait!' There was a small but noticeable pause before he added quietly, 'Please.'

Louise hesitated, one slender hand resting on the black button that would summon the lift. All she had to do was press it and take the lift up to her room, then she could put this whole unpleasant incident behind her. It wasn't as though she was under any obligation to help him. It had been purely out of the goodness of her heart that she had offered to do so in the first place. No one would blame her for walking away, not after the way he had spoken to her. So why was she standing there hesitating? Why did she find it quite so hard to leave? Because he'd said please? Or because, despite the coldness of his blue eyes and the lines of pain contorting his face, he was possibly the most devastatingly handsome man she'd ever seen?

The sheer irrationality of the thought brought her spinning round, her eyes wide, her creamy-tanned skin tinged with colour, and she was lost the very moment she saw him standing there, swaying perilously. She ran back across the room and looped his arm around her shoulders, steadying him with her far smaller frame when he almost fell. He was very tall, tall and well built, with powerful shoulders straining against the thin silk of his white shirt and a muscular chest that tapered down to a trim waist. It took all Louise's strength to hold him up as she wrapped her arm around the back of his waist as he took an unsteady step forwards.

'Slowly, now. Just take your time,' she murmured softly, using the very tone she'd used a thousand times before to a thousand different patients, only this time, instead of having a soothing effect, it seemed to have just the opposite.

'I am taking my time! I'm not in any fit state to do otherwise, am I? Perhaps you could control that irritating tendency you have to offer unnecessary advice, if it isn't too much to ask.'

Louise stiffened at the unpleasant note in the man's voice. Her fingers curled into the hard flesh at his waist, digging in deeper as her temper started to rise. 'I shall be delighted to if you'll agree to curb that foul temper of yours. Now come along. The sooner this is over with, obviously the happier we shall both be.'

She urged him forwards, closing her eyes to the rasping sound of his breathing, the burning heat of his body pressed against hers. He might be ill, but he wasn't going to get much sympathy from her, not after such ingratitude!

'If you could just get your fingers out of my ribs, then maybe I could breathe a bit better. And do you think you could slow down? It may have escaped your notice, but I'm not in any fit state to run the four-minute mile right now.'

He might be feeling ill, but obviously it hadn't affected his tongue! He could still summon up enough sarcasm to make her want to do something totally unprofessional! Louise glared up at him, her angry gaze tangling with his for no longer than a heartbeat before she looked away, feeling . . . well, shaken. All he'd done was glare back at her, his dark brows drawn together, his lips set into a thin, uncompromising line of displeasure. So why did she suddenly feel breathless, the blood singing along her veins? She must be more upset by his rudeness than she'd realised.

Annoyance ran through her and she slid out from beneath his arm, watching dispassionately as he made a grab for a nearby chair and hung on grimly. 'If you prefer to manage by yourself, then carry on. I can think of any number of more interesting ways to pass the evening than spending it helping an ungrateful, carping bore like you.'

His knuckles gleamed white from the effort of holding himself upright, but his eyes were deadly as they swept her angry face with icy contempt. 'I'm quite sure you can.' He smiled tightly, his lips drawing back from strong white teeth in an expression that held little sign of amusement. 'Far more interesting and far more lucrative, isn't that right? But while I hate to curtail your night-time activities, Miss Carter, I am forced to point out that you started this by poking your pretty little nose in in the first place. So may I suggest that you finish it? Look on it as the ideal opportunity to perfect that caring little act of yours.'

What did he mean? What act? And how could her evenings be classified as lucrative? Unless he'd seen her in the hotel's casino last night. She'd spent no more than ten dollars at the gaming tables, and that more to pass the time than out of any hope of winning. Perhaps he imagined that was how she usually passed her time. Either that or he was rambling from the fever he was running.

It was the thought of the fever that decided her. She caught his arm and draped it across her shoulders again as she started towards the lift. She might not like his attitude, but there was no way she could ignore six years of nursing experience and training. Until she could hand him over into some-one else's care he was her responsibility.

'Which room are you in?' She pressed the button to summon the lift, flexing her shoulders as he leant against the wall and closed his eyes as they waited for it to arrive.

'Seven-thirteen.'

Louise gasped in surprise. 'Why, that's next door to me.'

His eyes opened slowly, something glittering in their depths that chilled her to the bone. 'I know.'

How could he manage to make a simple statement sound like an accusation? And why should he want to? Just what did he have against her, apart from the fact that she'd made the mistake of smiling at him that morning and then offered to help him tonight?

Louise searched his face, but there was nothing there to supply an answer as he closed his eyes again and slumped against the wall. He groaned sud-denly, one large hand pressed flat to his stomach, a flush of colour tingeing his angular cheekbones, and she studied him in consternation.

'Look, I really do think you need a doctor. Let me see if I can find someone to call one out. You don't know what could be wrong with you.'

He shook his head, running his hand over his forehead to wipe away the beads of perspiration. 'No doctor. I don't need one.'

'Why? Because it might ruin the macho image to admit you're ill?' There was a sting to her words, and his eyes opened at once to centre disturbingly on her face.

'I don't need a doctor because I know exactly what is wrong with me. It has nothing whatsoever to do with image.' His eyes travelled the length of her slender body, lingering meaningfully on the simple lines of her cream dress with its delicate white lace collar before lifting back to hers with mockery in their depths. 'We don't all put on an act, Miss Carter, as you obviously do.'

Perhaps it was her own fault for starting it, but she didn't like the way he said that, nor the way he was looking at her! For a moment Louise battled with a desire to tell him exactly what she thought, before swallowing the heated words. It would achieve nothing to start an argument, only prolong this whole unpleasant episode, which was the last thing she wanted.

'What is wrong with you, then?' she asked quietly, ignoring the way one thick dark brow winged upwards with amusement when he realised she wasn't going to retaliate.

'Squid.'

'I beg your pardon?' She stared at him in astonishment.

He sighed deeply, running a hand through his hair to push it back from his damp forehead. 'I ate out tonight at a seafood restaurant. I specifically ordered that there should be no squid in the meal, but . . .' He shrugged, then grimaced faintly as he clutched his stomach again. 'I seem to be allergic to squid.'

'Yet you still took a chance by opting for that kind of meal? How could you have been so foolhardy? Surely you could taste the squid so why did you eat it?'

'No, I couldn't taste it. The fish was done in some kind of heavy sauce, and in fact I ended up leaving most of it, but obviously the damage had been done by then. I don't expect this sort of mistake to be made when I have given specific instructions to guard against it. However, that is immaterial now. I shall deal with the restaurant tomorrow.' He straightened with obvious effort as the lift arrived. 'Now if you have quite finished with the lectures as to what I should and shouldn't eat, is it too much to ask you to help me up to my room?'

A shiver ran through Louise as she took his arm, barely conscious of responding to the order. She wouldn't like to be in that chef's shoes tomorrow! Whoever he was, this man would be the wrong man to cross, so pity help the staff at that restaurant when he'd got through 'dealing' with them!

Within minutes they were outside his room. Louise steadied him against the wall, then took the key from his hand and unlocked the door, shooting a worried look at him when she felt the heat of his skin. Despite his temperature, she could see shivers racking his body, a sure sign that the allergic reaction had nowhere near run its course. Could she really in all conscience leave him alone with no one to help if he got worse?

She sighed as she opened the door and walked inside to switch on the lamps, casting a golden glow across the thick white carpet and white silken spread that covered the king-sized bed. His room was almost a duplicate of hers—huge, airy, the pale sea-green walls adding just the perfect hint of delicate

colour. She would give anything just to say goodnight, go to her own room, and enjoy the quiet
luxury but her infuriating conscience wouldn't allow
her to do that now that it was in full flight. The
man was ill, and she couldn't leave him; it went
against everything she'd ever been taught.

Decision made, she turned back to the door and
took his arm to help him over to the bed, watching
as he sank down on it with a sigh of weariness. He
was obviously feeling rotten, and it had probably
only been will-power that had kept him going this
long—that and a generous measure of sheer bad
temper. The very least she could do was try to make
him comfortable.

'Do you want me to help you into bed?' she offered quietly.

'No, I damned well don't! Look, Miss Carter,
perhaps you mean well. I'm willing to give you the
benefit of the doubt, but I would appreciate it if
you would just leave. Thank you for what you have
done, and rest assured that I shall see that you are
suitably reimbursed for your time and effort.'

She drew back as though he had struck her, her
eyes blazing at the insult. 'I don't want reim-
bursing! You can keep your money, Mr
Ungrateful!'

'And have you making some claim on me at a
later date? I don't think so. I know your type only
too well, and I'm not fool enough to leave myself
open like that.' His eyes closed and he sank back
against the pillows. 'Now just get out of here, will
you?'

There was a point when even the noisiest conscience should be silenced, and she had reached it.

Without another word, Louise turned on her heel and strode towards the door, every nerve tingling with fury. How dared he speak to her like that? Just who did he think he——?

'And don't slam the door when you leave!'

She paused at the sound of that harsh, deep voice, her hand resting lightly on the door-handle, her brow puckering into a small frown. How had he guessed what she'd been only vaguely contemplating? She glanced round at where he was lying on the bed, trying hard to recall any previous, if fleeting, feelings of compassion for what he must be suffering, but funnily enough they all seemed to have disappeared.

A rather malicious smile curved her generous mouth and she took a slow, invigorating breath... then slammed the door behind her as hard as she could, listening to the muttered curse that echoed after it with a quite unworthy feeling of satisfaction.

It might have been petty, it was definitely childish, but by heaven it made her feel a whole lot better!

It was the crash that woke her, the sharp, nerve-stretching sound of glass shattering.

Louise reached for the small travel clock and peered at the illuminated dial for several seconds before her brain could make sense of it. Two a.m. What an unearthly hour to be woken up.

She rolled over and glanced at the twin bed next to hers, not really surprised to see that it was empty. Obviously Carol hadn't come back yet, and who could blame her? Meeting Simon again like that on

the plane had been a heaven-sent opportunity for
her, and Louise wasn't selfish enough to resent her
friend making the most of it. It was just that it left
her out on a limb.

She sat up, pushing the silky dark curls back from
her face as she drew up her knees and rested her
forehead against the cool, smooth satin. She'd been
so excited about winning this holiday for two in
Miami; it had seemed like a dream come true. Two
weeks of luxury in a top-class hotel, all expenses
paid. She'd be nothing short of ungrateful if she
admitted that the hotel wasn't quite what she would
have chosen. It catered mainly for an older, wealthy
clientele, retired couples who enjoyed the quiet
luxury of the elegant surroundings. Of course it
would have been different if Carol had been around
more, but Simon had claimed most of her time since
they'd arrived, whisking her back to his hotel at
the other side of town.

Louise knew only too well how her friend felt
about him, having spent many unhappy evenings
over the past months with Carol pouring her heart
out to her. She was glad they had found each other
again, but she did sometimes wish it hadn't been
on this side of the Atlantic!

Still, she hadn't really been that lonely. Through
force of circumstance she'd made friends with a few
people who'd been on the same flight, and they'd
made it their business to see that she wasn't left on
her own all the time. It was just that she sometimes
longed for someone of her own age to talk to. Apart
from herself, Carol and the man in the next room
there was no one under the age of fifty in the hotel.

At the thought of the man she sat bolt upright, suddenly remembering the noise that had woken her. Had it come from his room? If so, what had happened?

She jumped out of bed and pressed her ear to the connecting wall between the two rooms, but there was no sound from the other side. Was he sleeping, or had the sound she'd heard been him falling as he'd got up, possibly to summon help? Despite his objections, she'd phoned down to the desk before she'd got into bed and requested that a doctor should call to see him, but had he been yet? Even now the man might be lying there, too weak to move.

There was no way she would sleep now with so many unanswered questions whirling inside her head, so she dragged on the silky blue robe that matched her gown and crept from her room to tap on his door, waiting with a mounting impatience for him to answer. She chewed on her lip, weighing the choices of calling Reception again to ask for help or leaving well alone. If he was asleep then he wouldn't welcome being disturbed, and frankly, she'd borne enough of his foul temper to last a lifetime, but if he was ill . . . ?

She turned to hurry back to her room and call the desk, then gasped when her foot caught on something sharp lying on the floor. She bent down to see what it was, then realised she might just have found the solution to the dilemma as she picked up the key. It must have fallen from the lock when she'd slammed the door before, and now it was just what she needed. She would take a quick look in his room, check he was all right, then leave.

The room was in darkness, just a faint glow from the window reflecting eerily off the mirrored vanity unit. Holding her breath, Louise crept towards the bed, neatly side-stepping the shattered remains of the Tiffany lamp that had been standing on the bedside table. That breaking must have been the sound that had woken her. Now if she could just check that he was all right, then she could leave.

He was lying on top of the bed, his long legs tangled up in the satin spread. He'd managed to undress down to a pair of dark boxer shorts, his muscular chest bare and gleaming like moulded bronze in the dim light. Louise felt a strange tightness in her chest as she stared down at the man's near-naked body, and it shocked her. She'd seen naked bodies, both male and female, more times than she could count, so what was different about him?

It was purely out of a desire to answer that question that she allowed her eyes to travel down from the wide shoulders and over that perfectly sculpted torso, then carry on across the slimness of his hips, the muscular hardness of his thighs and down the length of his legs to his large, well-shaped feet. It was *purely* a thirst for knowledge, not any desire simply to enjoy this embodiment of masculine perfection. There was no need for her to feel guilty when she looked up and saw that his eyes were open and he was watching her, but she did!

'What are you doing here?' His voice was hoarse, so low that she had to bend closer to hear him, and she found herself answering just as quietly.

'I heard a crash. I thought you might need help.'

'I knocked the lamp over.' He glanced sideways, his eyes faintly glazed as they turned back to her. 'I'm thirsty.'

He sounded so different now, his voice rasping softly, sensuously, as he uttered the plaintive statement. Louise felt something warm and almost tender flow through her. She smiled down at him, her eyes softening as she studied his flushed face, the beads of perspiration on his forehead and scattered among the dark hairs that covered his chest. 'No wonder. You're still running a temperature. Lie still and I'll get you something to drink.'

She hurried over to the small built-in fridge and sorted quickly through the contents until she found a bottle of mineral water. She poured some into a glass and carried it back to him, slipping an arm behind his shoulders to help him up so that he could drink. He took a few thirsty swallows before she took the glass away and set it down on the bedside table. 'That's enough for now. You don't want to make yourself sick.'

He grimaced as he sank against the pillows and ran a hand over his face. 'I doubt if I could be, not after the past couple of hours. I must have broken records for the number of times I've been sick, but the doctor said that it was the best thing that could happen.'

'So he did come, then?'

'Yes. I take it that you called him?' He sighed at her nod. 'There wasn't any need. He couldn't give me anything, just told me to drink as much fluid as I could. I just wish I didn't feel so damned hot.'

'You're bound to while your body is still fighting the effects of that squid.' Automatically she ran a hand down the firm muscles on his upper arm, testing the heat of his skin. 'You could do with sponging down.'

'If that's an offer, then I'll take you up on it.' He closed his eyes, looking so helpless for a moment that Louise barely stopped to consider what she was doing. She cast one quick glance at him, then hurried through to the bathroom and filled the basin to soak one of the washcloths in cool water. His eyes were still closed when she walked back into the bedroom, but they opened when she started to wipe the cloth over his face and down the strong column of his neck.

'That feels good,' he murmured huskily, his pale blue eyes so light and clear in the faint light from the window that they looked like washed silver. 'You have a marvellous touch, Miss Carter, although I imagine that there have been many men who've told you that.'

Her hand stilled for a second, her fingers resting lightly against the base of his neck, where she could feel a pulse tapping steadily. Had there been just the faintest hint of double meaning in that? But if so, what?

'Surely you're not shy about carrying on with your ministrations?'

The husky question woke her from the trance and her hand moved on, sliding the damp cloth across his shoulders, back and forth, taking the heat out of his skin. She forced the momentary unsettling thought to the back of her mind, smiling calmly down at him. 'No, I'm not shy. I must have done this hundreds of times, Mr...' She laughed faintly, suddenly conscious of how ludicrous the situation was. 'Do you know that I don't have any idea what your name is?'

'No?' He raised one dark brow in that mocking way she was learning to recognise, if not understand, then slowly his heavy lids lowered and he settled himself deeper into the pillows. 'Wyatt. That's my name. Wyatt.'

'Well, then, Mr Wyatt, just lie still and rest. There's no need to feel embarrassed about letting me help you. It's just a sensible precaution to lower that temperature of yours.'

'Oh, I'm not embarrassed, Miss Carter. Far from it. I'm sure that you are very experienced in this kind of thing. I shall enjoy reaping the benefits of that.'

The conversation was turning into a riddle, twisting and turning backwards and forwards so that she wasn't certain what he was saying. A frown puckered her brow, but she carried on sponging him down, her hands moving smoothly and confidently as she stroked the damp cloth over his skin time and again until the steady, measured sound of his breathing told her that he had fallen asleep.

She ran a hand lightly over his chest and shoulders, then felt his forehead with the back of her knuckles. He was much cooler now, his skin barely warmer than her own. Obviously it had done the trick, but she was well aware that his temperature could rise again very quickly, undoing all her good work. She'd wait a while to see how he was then.

She tossed the wet cloth on to the bedside table,
then went and sat down in the chair by the window
and ran a hand wearily over her face as tiredness
enveloped her. She yawned then grimaced, fighting
to keep her eyes open and not give in to the almost
overwhelming desire to fall asleep. There would be
time enough for that later, once she was sure that
he was all right. She could go back to her room
and sleep the clock round...

CHAPTER TWO

THIS time it was a knock at the door that disturbed her. Louise muttered crossly, keeping her eyes tightly closed as she tried to blot out the irritating sound.

'Can you get that if you're awake?'

The deeply masculine voice roused her in a trice. She sat bolt upright, then groaned as her head spun with dizziness. For a blank second she stared down at the chair she was sitting in, then looked round the room she'd been using for almost a week now, confused by the strangeness of it all. Why was the door suddenly on the opposite side of the room? And surely that picture above the tall chest of drawers had been of flowers last time she'd looked, not birds?

Puzzled, her eyes moved on, taking stock of the furnishings, the huge double bed... Her heart leapt into her throat, beating so hard that for a moment she was afraid she would suffocate. Slowly, reluctantly, her gaze slid back to the satin bedspread and travelled across it inch by disbelieving inch. There wasn't a double bed in her room, so where was she?

The question was quickly followed by the answer—approximately six feet of answer, to be precise. For a stunned minute Louise just stared at the man who emerged from the bathroom, a white towel fastened low around his lean hips. Then in a fast, heart-shaking sweep her eyes ran from the top of his damp black hair to the tips of his naked feet before coming back to rest helplessly on his face.

'The door,' he repeated slowly, and icily. 'Do you think you can answer it?'

'I...' Louise scrambled to her feet, staring blankly round the room, and heard him mutter something uncomplimentary as he strode past her. She ran a trembling hand over her hot face, trying to make sense of what was happening, and almost groaned aloud as she remembered the events of the previous night. How could she have been so *careless* as to let herself fall asleep like that?

'Surprise! Wyatt, darling, I *know* I should have called first, but I was just dying to see you, so... here I am!'

The breathlessly eager note in the woman's voice made Louise wince with embarrassment, although she knew that she was in no position to criticise. She took a slow breath and forced herself to turn towards the door, studying the vision of female beauty who stood framed in its opening. Perfect blonde hair, perfect smooth, pale skin, perfect tailored white trousers and navy spotted blouse, everything about the woman was perfect—too perfect, in fact. She looked like a mannequin as she stood there, resting one slender pink-tipped hand on the man's bare shoulder as she smiled up at him.

'You don't really mind me coming, do you, darling?' Her voice dropped a note, openly seductive now.

'It might have been better if you'd called, Carling.' He glanced over his shoulder, his eyes fastening on Louise with a touch of deliberation in the look. 'It isn't the most convenient of times for a surprise visit.'

'Not convenient . . . ?' The woman's gaze followed his, her eyes widening when they came to rest on Louise standing by the side of the tumbled bed. In a fast, almost disbelieving curve, they ran across the rumpled satin spread, then over Louise's body in the pale blue gown and robe, and Louise decided there and then to nip whatever ideas the stranger was getting in the bud.

She pushed her ruffled hair back from her face, forcing a polite smile as she took a step towards the couple, who were standing close together by the door. 'Hello,' she said softly. 'I know this must seem awfully——'

'Darling, you don't have to explain. Carling understands about these things.' The man's voice was smooth as silk as he moved away from the woman and started back across towards Louise, yet his eyes held a hard glint that robbed Louise of the ability to speak for a moment. Confused, she stared back at him, then gasped as he slid an arm around her shoulder and pulled her closer so that she could feel the warmth of his big body all down the side of her breast and hip, smell the clean fragrance of soap that clung to his skin. The sensations made her feel almost giddy by their very unfamiliarity, and he took full advantage of the moment. His hand slid under her chin, warm and firm as he tilted her face and stared into her startled eyes for a moment then bent and kissed her hard on the mouth.

When he raised his head Louise couldn't have spoken to save her life, too stunned by what he'd done and the effect one kiss could have. She'd been kissed before many times, but she couldn't remember ever feeling as though her heart was going to beat itself to pulp inside her chest.

She breathed slowly, willing herself to find the strength to handle this unexpected twist, but didn't have time to utter a single word before the man continued in that same smooth-as-silk tone, 'I think I should introduce you two ladies, don't you?' He laughed softly, intimately, as his arm clasped Louise's shoulders even tighter. 'Louise, darling, I'd like you to meet Carling Hutton. Her father owns this hotel and the rest of the chain I'm negotiating to buy at present. Carling ... my fiancée, Louise Carter.'

She couldn't have felt more stunned if he'd hit her! Louise just stared at him, her eyes black with shock, before suddenly coming to her senses. This whole episode was fast turning into one of those Whitehall farces her parents had used to love so much: all it would need now was an irate husband with a shot-gun bursting into the room to complete the scene! But if he thought that she was going along with whatever he was plotting he could think again!

She pulled away from him, her face flushed with colour. 'Look, I've no idea what you think you're doing, but——'

He smiled as he pressed a long finger against her lips to stem the heated flow of words. 'I know, I know, honey. I shouldn't have said anything about our engagement until we've had time to tell your parents the marvellous news, but Carling is a trusted friend. She wouldn't dream of letting the cat out of the bag and spoiling the surprise. Would you, Carling?'

There was a momentary pause, then the woman spoke, a smile pasted to her pink-tinted lips. 'Of course not, Wyatt. You know I wouldn't dream of doing anything to spoil your... happiness. Congratulations to you both. I must admit this has come as a bit of a surprise. I don't know how you managed to keep your... friendship with Miss Carter from the Press, Wyatt. They're usually keen to keep abreast of what the great Wyatt Lord gets up to.'

There was just the faintest trace of scepticism in the woman's voice, but Louise was less concerned with that than the fact that not only did she suddenly have a fiancé, but that she hadn't even known his real name. Wyatt Lord. She rolled the name round and round as she studied his handsome face, the clean-cut lines of his profile, but she couldn't ever remember hearing of him before.

'I think the Press have started to give up on me lately.' He laughed deeply, catching Louise's hand to twine his fingers with hers. 'I've been a bit of a recluse over recent months, and I have this little lady to thank for that.'

Louise winced at the endearment and tried to snatch her hand away. She was nobody's 'little lady', and especially not his, and it was about time she made that clear! 'Look, this has gone on long enough, don't you think? I have no idea what——'

Once again he stopped her, pulling her into his arms to hold her so close that she could barely breathe as he kissed her with punishing hardness,

his eyes glittering a warning as he stared down at
her. 'You mustn't be embarrassed, honey. I know
this isn't the way we planned it to happen, but...'
He shrugged lightly, his arms dropping to loop
around the back of her waist and keep her pressed
tightly against him as he looked over her head at
Carling. Louise could feel every inch of his muscular chest through the thin fabric of her robe and
gown, could feel the dampness of the towel that
covered his hips, the strength of his thighs where
they touched hers, and her mouth went dry at the
sheer intimacy of what he was doing. Kisses and a
little light lovemaking she'd experienced and could
handle, but this... this was something way beyond
her limited experience!

She barely heard him when he carried on
speaking, too busy trying to cope with the mul-
titude of mixed emotions she was feeling: embarrassment, anger and a strange heady languor, a
feeling that she wanted to stay in his arms, pressed
against his powerful body, forever...

Her head jerked up, her face flaming at the
thought, and she suddenly came to her senses in
time to hear him say softly, 'I'm afraid that nature
took care of the rest. We didn't mean to pre-empt
our wedding night, but after all Louise's tender care
last night when I was so ill... I'm sure you understand, Carling, don't you? And don't feel that
Louise should be feeling embarrassed or ashamed
of what happened this morning.'

Oh, enough was enough! She might not have followed the conversation from start to finish, but it
didn't take a genius to work out what he'd been
telling the other woman. If he imagined that she

was going to allow Carling to leave this room thinking that she and Wyatt Lord had slept together, then he could think again.

Louise tried again to set the record straight, only this time it was Carling who stopped her. She moved across the room, her mouth curved into a smile of understanding that did little to disguise the hatred burning in her green eyes as she stared back at Louise. Close to, she was younger than Louise had imagined she was, the skilful make-up and polished appearance lending her a sophistication more suited to someone in her late twenties. Louise would put her age at less than that—nineteen, possibly twenty, but no more.

'Of course not! Wyatt's right, Louise, you shouldn't feel at all uncomfortable about me coming up here and finding you in his room.'

Why did that bland, polite statement make her feel like squirming? Louise had no idea, just the sure and certain knowledge that that had been Carling Hutton's intention. Anger raced through her, stealing away the ability to think rationally and weigh up her actions, to see them as the folly they undoubtedly were. 'Thank you, Carling. I may call you that, I hope?' She pouted gently, then let her hands trail up Wyatt Lord's chest, her nails tangling in the thick curls of hair as she twisted one slowly and, she hoped, lovingly around her finger as she stared up at him with the most limpidly besotted expression she could muster. 'It's good to know that you have such understanding friends, darling. I'm sure Carling and I will find a lot in common once we get to know one another better.'

His eyes were murderous as he grasped her wandering hand and held it so hard that Louise had to bite back a moan of pain. 'I'm sure you will, my love. However, now isn't really the time to start building on that friendship. I'm sure Carling will understand if we cut short this meeting.'

'Of course.' Carling laughed lightly, a tinkly sound that grated on Louise's nerves. 'I'm sure Louise is just dying for me to leave so that she can get showered and changed.' She shuddered delicately as she smoothed a hand over her perfect blonde mane of hair. 'There's nothing worse than being caught out, is there, Louise?'

Up until then Louise had barely spared a thought for her appearance; now she was suddenly achingly conscious of the tumbled state of her dark curls, the naked shine of her bare face, the creases in the blue gown and robe she'd fallen asleep in. She lifted a hand to smooth one stray curl back from her face, then dropped it again as she saw the expression of triumph on the other girl's face. As Carling swept towards the door she paused in the doorway. 'So I'll leave you to get sorted out now. Don't forget that we're expecting you tonight, Wyatt. And Louise, of course. Daddy is going to be thrilled when I tell him about your engagement. I'm sure he will want to organise some sort of a party while you're with us on Paradise. *Ciao.*'

The door closed softly, the sound echoing almost painfully in the sudden silence. Louise took one long deep breath, then another for good measure, then pushed herself out of Wyatt Lord's arms.

'I don't know what that was all about, Mr Lord,' she began stormily, twin spots of colour burning

angrily in her cheeks, 'and I don't think I really
want to know! I just want to tell you that I have
never...*never*...been so...so...insulted in the
whole of my life!'

'No?' He raised a mocking brow, his eyes cold
as they skimmed her flushed face. 'If you carry on
living the way you have been, then I'm sure time
will remedy that.'

He turned to walk back through to the bathroom,
but Louise caught his arm, her fingers leaving white
pressure marks against his tanned skin. 'And what
do you mean by that? Look, you've done nothing
but throw veiled insults at me since we met, but
why?'

'I think this discussion can wait until I'm dressed,
don't you?'

She hung on tightly, her face burning with anger
as she glared back at him. 'It's not waiting for anything! Understand? I spent the best part of the night
here taking care of you, and all I get for my pains
is insults, and I want to know why. The same as I
want to know what you thought you were doing
telling that woman that we...we...'

She couldn't quite bring herself to say the words,
but he had none of her reservations. 'Slept
together? Come on, why put on this little act?
Outraged virginal modesty sits oddly on your
shoulders, Louise. Why pretend that we don't both
know what you're up to here in this hotel?' He held
her gaze for a second, then removed the towel from
around his hips, smiling coldly at her shocked gasp
as he strode naked as the day he was born to the
wardrobe and pulled out underwear and jeans and
a pale blue T-shirt.

He stepped into a pair of white boxer shorts, watching her steadily as he drew them up around his slim hips. 'What, no more maidenly protests? Of course not. You've probably seen more men naked than a dozen women would see in their lifetime, isn't that right? So let's stop all this play-acting, shall we?'

Too late Louise realised that she'd been standing there staring at him. She spun round, closing her eyes as she tried to compose herself again, but all she could see behind her closed lids was a picture of Wyatt Lord standing there naked, his broad chest tanned under the thick pelt of hair, his hips paler than the rest of his body. She swallowed down a soft moan of protest, then turned round to face him again, knowing that somehow they had to sort this mess out.

'Yes, I've seen men naked before, but that doesn't mean that I appreciate your acting this way. I don't know what I've done to deserve this sort of treatment, Mr Lord; I don't really care. All I want is for you to set the record straight and tell Carling Hutton the truth.'

He zipped the jeans, then pulled the T-shirt over his head, finger-combing the thick, glossy strands of black hair back into place. 'That is something I have no intention of doing. I'm quite happy to have her think that she interrupted a tender little scene here in this room.'

'But why?' Louise ran a shaking hand over the creased folds of the thin blue robe, her fingers worrying the soft fabric. 'I just don't understand any of this, not what you told that woman, nor all the horrible things you keep on saying to me.'

'The truth hurts, eh? It's easier just to pass off what you're doing without really thinking about it, isn't it?' His eyes traced her slender body with open contempt. 'You are a beautiful woman, Louise, but you don't need me to tell you that. You are well aware of your own charms, and use them.'

'I don't know what you mean.'

'No? Then explain to me why you are staying in this hotel, a hotel that caters for a clientele far older than you. You must be...what, twenty-three... four?' At her nod he continued, 'Are you really here just to enjoy a holiday in luxurious and *peaceful* surroundings, as the hotel brochure boasts? Or are you here to use that beauty of yours to ensnare some rich old man who'll provide you with the luxury you want from life?'

'What? No!' Horrified, she stared back at him. 'You've got it wrong! I can't imagine where you got such a ridiculous idea from!'

'Can't you? Not so ridiculous when I have seen and heard evidence to back up every word I just said.'

'What evidence? What are you talking about?'

He folded his arms and leant easily against the wardrobe. 'You should be more careful, Louise, if you hope to maintain this pretence of innocence. You forget that our rooms adjoin and that sound carries through the walls.' He raised a dark brow, then continued when she made no attempt to speak. 'The day I moved into this room I heard you—how shall I put it delicately?—entertaining a gentleman friend. Monday, it was. Then there's been all the frequent comings and goings to your room at odd hours, coincidentally by a gentleman of advanced

years. I heard him talking about you by the pool
the other day. It was most enlightening. He was
most complimentary about your sensitive hands and
your touch like an angel, if I remember his words
correctly.' He shook his head so that the light from
the window bounced flashes of blue fire off its raven
darkness. 'I never imagined that it was possible to
come up with so many glowing compliments, but
he managed it. He seems truly besotted, so all it
needs now is for you to choose your time and then
get him well and truly hooked.'

Louise stared at him in dumb silence when he
stopped speaking, her mind racing in a dozen different directions as it made sense out of what he'd
said, but a far different sense than he'd made!

The man he was talking about, a certain Mr
Holden, had fallen and cut his leg badly on the way
to the airport. Louise had sat next to him and his
wife on the flight over and offered to change the
dressings when his wife had confessed that she hated
the sight of blood! The cut had been healing nicely,
thanks to her attentions and the frequent changes
of dressings.

It was such an innocent explanation to a far from
innocent accusation, leaving only the mystery of
her 'entertaining' in her room, and that could be
explained very simply: Carol and Simon. Louise
had found them in the room when she'd got back
from a solo sightseeing tour on Monday, and had
steadfastly turned a blind eye to their rapturous
expressions!

It was all so simple to explain in just a few brief
sentences, yet, looking at Wyatt Lord, Louise knew
without the shadow of a doubt that he would never

believe her. He seemed determined to see her in the worst light possible, although for the life of her she couldn't understand why.

'Look, Mr Lord, you seem to have got an entirely wrong impression here.'

'Wyatt.' He stood up straight, flexing the heavy muscles in his shoulders. 'You may as well get used to calling me that right from the start. And to answer your statement, Louise, I don't think I've got anything wrong. On the contrary I can see quite clearly what's been going on here in this hotel.'

He was so pigheadedly arrogant! He'd formed this ridiculous opinion of her, and nothing, not even the truth, was going to make him change his mind. Louise drew herself up to her full five feet five and glared back at him. 'I can see it's pointless trying to talk to you. You're entitled to your opinions, but it's just a pity if they are the wrong ones.' She started to walk past him, stopping abruptly when he caught her arm. 'Do you mind?' she demanded haughtily, staring down at his large hand fastened around her forearm. 'I want to go back to my room. This discussion is over and done with as far as I'm concerned.'

He nodded agreement, but made no attempt to free her. 'If you mean that you've accepted that it's pointless to keep on with that little pretence of innocence, then that's correct. However, there are other matters we need to discuss right now, Louise, namely our rather abrupt engagement.'

She froze, her eyes locked on the darkness of his skin against the pale creamy tan of her own before they lifted to meet his. 'Pardon?'

'I think you heard me all right.'

'Oh, I heard, it's just the understanding I'm
having difficulty with.' She twisted her arm, but
achieved little apart from bruising her flesh. Anger
rose hot and swift as it rode on the wake of the
pain, and she glared at him. 'Watch my lips, *Mister*
Lord, then perhaps you will understand what I am
saying: we are not engaged! I don't know what sort
of a game you were playing just now and I don't
really care. Now let me go.'

'Not yet. Not until you understand what I am
saying.' He pushed her back so that she sat down
abruptly on the bed, towering in front of her as he
glared down into her furious face. 'I have told
Carling Hutton that we are engaged, and that is
what I intend her to believe. I am in the middle of
negotiations to buy this chain of hotels from
Carling's father, and I don't intend for anything to
disrupt that! Unfortunately, though, Carling has
been getting ideas that she and I would make the
perfect couple, ideas that her father would be only
too delighted to go along with. Carling is the apple
of his eyes; what she wants she gets, and pity help
the man who crosses her. I want these hotels to add
to the others I own, and I intend to have them, but
I don't intend to pay the ultimate price by marrying
Carling. That's where you come in.'

'Me? You really imagine that I would agree to
go along with this deception?' She laughed harshly,
watching the way his face tightened and his pale
eyes turned to silver ice. 'No way, Mr Lord. I don't
care what you do, but there is no way on God's
green earth that I can be persuaded to act as
your fiancée.'

'You think not?' He stepped closer, his eyes meeting hers and holding. 'Not even to save yourself from the embarrassment of being thrown out of this hotel?'

'Thrown out?' She shot to her feet, pushing past him to stand against the wall as though she needed its solid support.

'Mmm, could be a bit of a problem, I imagine, especially if I contact a few other hotels and warn them of the circumstances surrounding your abrupt departure from here.'

'I...I... That's ridiculous! I don't care who you are, but you can't do that! I won't let you blackmail me into going along with your stupid plan!' Was that really her voice sounding so shrill? Louise bit her lip as she tried to hang on to the last of her composure. Back at the hospital her control was legendary; she'd never been known even to raise her voice, let alone have hysterics, as seemed likely now. But back at the hospital there hadn't been Wyatt Lord as provocation!

'Oh, but I can. I can do everything I threaten, Louise. Have no doubt of that. Apart from the fact that I own several chains of hotels in this town and throughout Florida, I also have interests in quite a few others. If I made it known that you are un-welcome, then you wouldn't find another room. Then of course there is always the possibility that the manager here might consider it his duty to inform the police about your activities.' He smiled faintly as he watched her. 'There has been a cam-paign recently to clean up this town by the vice squad, so I don't imagine they would look kindly upon what you've been doing.'

He spoke quietly, the words dropping almost gently into the stunned silence, yet the ripples they caused seemed like tidal waves.

'I haven't been doing anything! And I can get the man you referred to up here this minute to vouch for that!'

'I'm sure you can. He would be only too happy to corroborate any story you came up with rather than admit the truth in front of his wife, isn't that right? But you and I both know what the truth is, and unless you agree then the manager is going to hear it too.' He picked up the phone, watching her closely. 'I wonder what people will make of this back home in England?' He paused deliberately. 'You must have friends and possibly family there, Louise. A story like this is bound to hit the papers on both sides of the Atlantic, especially if you are deported, which most probably will happen.'

Deported? She closed her eyes, a mental picture of her parents springing to life. Her father had just applied for the headship of the local high school, while her mother had recently taken over the chair of the local Women's Circle. Then there was her brother, Paul, just starting out as a solicitor, not to mention her sister, Helen, just finishing her year's residency at the same hospital where Louise worked. She was innocent as the day, but the mud would stick to all of them!

She was so angry that she could barely speak. 'You would really do that? No, don't bother. I can see you would. You are the most despicable man

I've ever met, and I wish to heaven that I'd left you here to suffer by yourself last night!'

'But you didn't, did you? And why not? Because you thought there might be something in it for you? All right, then, Louise, I'd hate to disappoint you, so let me make you an offer. Lawrence Hutton has invited me to stay at his house in the Bahamas—on Paradise Island, to be precise. You will accompany me as my fiancée. That should effectively put paid to any ideas about my marrying into the family, yet guarantee that I get what I want.'

'And what do I get out of all this?' She smoothed the lace at the cuff of her robe, feeling anger churning inside her. It was hard to believe that anyone could be as coldly ruthless as Wyatt Lord was. She didn't doubt that he would carry out his threat, but if he thought she'd go along with him then he was in for a shock!

He set the phone back down with a satisfied smile that made her itch to reach out and slap his arrogant face, but she stopped herself. 'I'm glad you're being sensible about this. I thought you would once I had time to convince you that you could turn this to your advantage. In return for your help I shall sign an undertaking to let this whole matter drop, plus I'm willing to pay you a generous fee as compensation for not being able to reap the benefits of all your recent hard work. Understand?'

Oh, she did. She understood it all quite clearly, from A to Z, with every letter filled in along the way! What she *should* do now was laugh in his face and tell him to do his worst, challenge him to carry out all his miserable threats. So how was it that she

opened her mouth and heard with a sense of total
disbelief herself saying softly, 'How much?' *That*
was something she still couldn't understand prop-
erly even hours later!

CHAPTER THREE

THE ground fell away as the plane took to the skies. Louise held her breath, only releasing it as the plane gained its correct altitude and started to level off. She'd never flown in anything smaller than a 747 before, so this was a whole new experience, one she wasn't sure she liked.

She glanced sideways at Wyatt Lord, who was piloting the small Cessna, watching the way his hands moved confidently on the controls. It was obvious that he was as confident about flying as he appeared to be about everything else he did, and gradually she began to relax, although that did little to ease the knots in her stomach. She must have been mad to agree to this, stark, raving mad!

She looked away, shading her eyes against the glare from the vivid blue sky as she tried again to work out why she'd done such a crazy thing as to agree to this trip. Had it been merely those threats he'd uttered, threats that had made her feel more recklessly angry than she'd felt before in her life? She still wasn't one hundred per cent certain, but suddenly all Carol's dire warnings came rushing back to haunt her, and she had to bite her lip to stem the tiny moan.

'If you're going to be sick, then use one of the bags in the door pocket.'

If she'd thought for a moment that he'd said that out of concern, then she might have appreciated it,

41

but she wasn't fool enough to think that! The anger rose again, hot and swift, and strangely comforting, as she turned to stare coldly at him. 'Don't worry. I wasn't about to throw up all over your precious plane.'

He adjusted the controls, his face set as he shot her a quick glance. 'Then what is bothering you? Having second thoughts already?' He smiled, his mouth curling contemptuously beneath the heavy black moustache, his eyes hidden behind the mirrored glasses. 'I wouldn't waste my time if I were you. We made a deal, Louise, and I have every intention of seeing that you stick to it.'

'Second thoughts about earning myself ten thousand dollars?' She pretended to make a few rapid calculations on her fingers, her expression as avaricious as she could make it. 'What's that, about five and a half thousand pounds in sterling?' She laughed huskily, stretching her slender body like a cat who had been shown a saucer of cream, before settling back in the seat with a contented sigh. 'An offer like that doesn't come a girl's way very often.'

'But how long will the money last?' He removed his glasses, studying the elegant lines of her beige silk shirt and trousers, the smooth leather of her neat flat shoes. 'Clothes like those cost money, a lot of money. You'll be through that cash in next to no time, and then what will you do? Start looking for some other poor man to keep you?'

Louise ran a hand over the soft silk, smiling faintly to herself. The clothes she owned *were* expensive, but she hadn't bought them; the salary she earned was adequate to live on, but would never have stretched to designer labels. She was fortunate enough to have a cousin who was a buyer for a large store in Manchester, who was a clothesaholic. Jessica bought more outfits than she could hope to wear, then passed them on to Louise for a fraction of their cost when she tired of them. It was an arrangement that suited them both, but one she had no intention of telling Wyatt Lord about!

He slid the glasses back on, his jaw rigid as he banked the plane slowly then checked the panel before he spoke again. 'I think that the thing that's bothering you most is that someone has sussed your little game. It must be galling to have come so close then to lose out at the last moment.'

'Lose out on what?' She brushed a shiny dark curl from her eyes, then felt in her soft leather bag for her own sunglasses. Up here the sky was almost painfully bright, the sun blinding as it shone through the cockpit windscreen. She could feel the beginnings of a headache pressing at her temples, a sure sign that tiredness and anger had taken their toll.

'Hooking yourself that guy back at the hotel.' He laughed unpleasantly. 'He seemed fairly well set up, although I imagine you could have found someone a lot richer if you'd gone further afield. Miami is full of men like that who would be flattered by the attentions of a beautiful woman like you, Louise. Perhaps I've done you a favour by persuading you to come on this trip. It means you can always go back once we're through and try again for a bigger fish, one whose bank balance will last a while longer until you drain it dry.'

She was glad of the glasses. They shielded her eyes, so that he could not see how much that hurt.

How could she go through with this and spend the next week in the company of someone who despised her as much as he did?

Unexpected tears stung her eyes, but she blinked them away, refusing to admit even to herself how much it hurt to hear him say such horrible things. However, he was relentless, seemingly taking pleasure out of being as unpleasant as possible to her. 'Nothing to say? No girlish protestations about your innocence now? You disappoint me, Louise, you really do. I thought you'd be determined to keep on with the little charade you've been playing.'

She didn't bother turning to look at him, her voice slightly muffled as she held back a sob. 'What would be the point? You've made up your mind about me, and that's that. Why waste my breath?'

He caught her chin, forcing her head round to study her before he let her go abruptly. Louise drew in a shaky breath, clenching her hands to stop herself from rubbing her fingers along her jaw to wipe away the burning, disturbing imprint he'd left on her skin. She felt shaken by the brief contact, but why? It didn't make any sense.

'What made you start this in the first place, Louise?' His hands moved on the controls, firm and confident as they steadied the small plane as it lifted on a current of warm air. Below them Louise could see the sea, turquoise-blue, glistening in the hot sunlight. It was like a picture-postcard view, and at another time she would have taken pleasure from it, but right now all she could concentrate on was coping with Wyatt Lord's deliberate cruelty.

She shrugged dismissively, feigning a sophistication that was purely on the surface. Inside it felt
as though tiny daggers were being stabbed one by
one into her heart. 'Why does anyone decide on a
course of action? You weigh up the pros and cons,
then make the decisions. It's as simple as that.'

'Simple?' He laughed deeply, shaking his head
as he glanced sideways at her. 'You see this kind
of life you're leading as simple? Come on! You're
not a fool. You understand the risks, surely?'

'What risks? From where I'm sitting it all looks
fine to me. I find myself a rich . . . benefactor, then
live the life I've always longed for. Isn't that what
I'm doing?'

'And what about your family? Have they any
idea what you're up to?'

Definitely not! If her parents ever found out
about this they'd be horrified, not because they'd
believe that she was in America looking for a rich
sugar-daddy, but because she'd gone off with a
virtual stranger! The thought of their love
strengthened the determination that had kept her
going throughout the time she'd been packing at
the hotel while fielding Carol's protests. This man
had insulted her in a way that no one had ever done
before, and she was determined to make him pay
for every unpleasant word! She would go through
with this plan, even accept the money he paid
her . . . then take great satisfaction from throwing it
back in his arrogant face as she told him in terms
he couldn't doubt how very wrong he'd been. The
thought of watching Wyatt Lord squirm as he was
forced to apologise would see her through!

'No,' she said softly, just the faintest tremor of
distress in her voice, which she felt quite proud of.
'They...they've no idea what I'm doing right now.'

'Then why do it? You're a beautiful and intel-
ligent woman. You have other options, so why do
something your family would feel ashamed of if
they found out?'

'Money. Isn't that the key to understanding why,
Mr Lord? You said it yourself only this morning,
worked out very cleverly what I was doing in the
hotel and why.' She smiled airily, watching him
through the tinted lenses, enjoying the way his big
body stiffened at her open mockery.

'Yes, I worked it out. It wasn't difficult. I've seen
it happen before, watched men who make fools of
themselves over women like you, women who don't
give a damn about anything as long as they get what
they want. You should carry a health warning,
Louise, because you destroy lives!'

His anger was almost tangible, filling the con-
fines of the small plane, adding a new dimension
to the conversation that startled her.

'That sounds as though you're speaking from
personal experience. Did some woman take *you* for
a ride?'

He laughed harshly, such contempt in the sound
that it destroyed the last vestiges of amusement she
felt. 'No. I'm not fool enough to let any woman
do that to me. Oh, women have their uses, I'll
admit, but those are purely physical, and that's all
I'm interested in.'

She felt suddenly cold, despite the heat from the
sun, her skin tingling with an icy chill that stemmed
from deep inside. How could anyone sound as

totally devoid of feelings as he had? In some indefinable way, it shocked her almost as much as when he'd made those ridiculous accusations against her.

Suddenly she didn't want to continue with this disturbing conversation a moment longer, and cast round for something to say to fill the uncomfortable silence. 'How long will it be before we land now?'

'About twenty minutes or so, depending on how many other planes are due at the island.' He checked his watch, a faint mocking curl to his mouth, as though he understood her reasons for wanting to move the conversation along different channels. 'The airstrip at Paradise Island is purely that, a strip for the benefit of people who have houses there.'

'I see.' She turned to stare out of the side-window, forcing herself to push the unsettling exchange to the back of her mind. She wasn't interested in digging deeper, in trying to discover what had made Wyatt so cold and unfeeling. It wasn't any of her business, and she had to remember that and not allow natural curiosity to draw her into something she might come to regret. 'What are all those islands down there? There must be hundreds of them, some so tiny they're little more than a few rocks, I imagine.'

'They are. There are about seven hundred islands plus over two thousand cays down there that form the Bahamas, most of them so flat they are barely a hundred feet above sea-level at their highest points.'

'Good heavens! I never realised there were so many!' Astonished by the information, Louise turned back to the view, following the scattering of land in the deep turquoise sea, like jewels glistening against satin. 'Are they all inhabited?'

'No. Some of the smaller cays are privately owned, but most of them are uninhabited. There are no rivers or streams on any of the islands, so fresh water can be a problem. What little there is is usually found close to the surface, resting on salt water, so if wells are dug too deeply it can taste brackish and be quite unpalatable.

'If you look down there to your right you'll see New Providence Island, where the capital of the Bahamas, Nassau, is situated.'

Louise followed his directions, leaning over so that she could see better, but it was hard to distinguish the island through the haze of sun bouncing off the water. 'Do you mean there?' she queried, pointing to a spot to their right, then nearly jumped out of her skin when he caught her hand in his and moved it a fraction further, holding it steady as he guided her pointing finger. Heat ran along her veins so swiftly, so fiercely, that she caught her breath at the sheer unexpectedness of the sensation. Just for a moment her eyes lifted to meet his, and she wished that she could see the expression in them, but with the mirrored glasses firmly in place that was impossible.

'Can you see where I mean?' Was it her imagination, or had that deep voice softened slightly, the cutting note dulled just a fraction? Louise almost held her breath as she nodded quickly, afraid to speak and break this fragile moment of truce. How would it feel to have Wyatt Lord speak to her in that tone all the time, to hear warmth not ice in those deep rich tones, to see those pale eyes filled with something other than contempt?

'Paradise Island is just across the bay from Nassau Town. In fact it's linked to it by a bridge.' He let her hand drop abruptly as he focused his attention once more on the instrument panel. Louise let out the pent-up breath, feeling the heat slowly fading, leaving behind it a strange ache of regret. Wyatt Lord would never change his opinion of her; he would never look at her and see her for what she was. He'd made up his mind, and no matter if she did finally make him apologise for his mistake; it would be too late.

Somehow it seemed imperative that he shouldn't guess how she felt, so she forced herself to continue with the conversation, unaware that her soft voice held a note of pain it was impossible to disguise. 'Is Paradise Island as big as New Providence?'

He glanced at her, studying her face for a few seconds that made her feel strangely vulnerable, before he answered. 'No. It's barely seven-hundred-odd acres, mainly given over to tourism now, although years ago the settlers of New Providence used it to keep their pigs on.'

'Pigs?'

'Mmm, it was called Hog Island way back then, until it started to be developed in the 1950s as a resort. Now it boasts some fine hotels and a casino, plus quite a number of privately owned properties.'

'You seem to know an awful lot about the area. Do you have a house here?' It was just an innocent question, meant more to keep the conversation flowing along impersonal lines. It surprised her to see the way his hands tightened on the column, the way a nerve ticked heavily in his jaw.

'Not any longer. That went many years ago.'

The icy note was back with a vengeance, chilling her so that she unconsciously huddled deeper into the seat. 'Went? You mean it was sold?'

'Yes. My father sold it.' He paused, and Louise had the feeling that he was lost in some bitter thoughts of the past, before he made an obvious effort to draw himself back to the present. 'Does that disappoint you, Louise?'

She shook her head, making the silky curls dance around her head. 'No, why should it?'

'Oh, I just thought that you might be weighing up your prospects here.'

'What prospects? Why do you always talk in riddles?' She sat up, a warning *frisson* tingling along her veins.

'They are only riddles to those who don't want to admit the truth. Be honest for once in your life, Louise, and admit that you've been sitting there wondering if you could turn this enforced trip to your advantage.'

'I thought it already was to my advantage.' She sounded husky, a strange unease knotting her throat. 'I'm getting a free holiday in this tropical paradise, plus several thousand pounds in my pocket when I leave.'

'But how much better would it be if you managed to make a real killing while you're here?' He raised one thick dark brow as he slipped the glasses off and studied her closely, a faint question in the depth of his pale eyes. 'I'm not a vain man, Louise, but I'm not unaware of my own attractions.' He paused deliberately, letting the words lie between them like a barrier that it seemed impossible for her to cross. 'Shall I list them for you? Do I have to? I've seen the way you've been watching me while we've been flying down here, and it doesn't take much to understand what's behind all those looks.'

How she longed to find something cutting to say, something so sharply witty that he would shrivel at her feet! But typically she couldn't find anything apart from a rather wobbly, 'No!'

'I'm glad you're being sensible and admitting it. It will make life that much simpler for both of us if we lay our cards on the table.'

'I meant, no, you're wrong! I wasn't watching you.' The words came out in a rush as she tried to convince him, but she failed miserably.

He laughed, the sound echoing above the throbbing note of the engine. 'You don't back down, I'll give you that much. You're determined to play the innocent until the bitter end, but we shall be coming in to land soon and I want this sorted out.

'I am a rich man, Louise, a great deal richer than that guy you'd set your sights on in the hotel. However, I brought you with me for one reason only and, while I wouldn't be averse to you practising your seductive little wiles on me, I may as well make it plain that I have no intention of falling into your clutches.' He picked up the glasses, but just held them as he watched her steadily, watching the soft flush of colour running up her cheeks. 'To be blunt, honey, I'm quite willing to take you into my bed, but I don't intend to pay for the honour by becoming your next meal-ticket.'

'I ... Don't flatter yourself! I wouldn't have you in my bed if you came gift-wrapped!'

He smiled almost gently at her shocked denial, but there was nothing gentle about his expression as he leant over and caught her chin while he took her mouth in a bruising kiss that left her shaking.

'Gift-wrapped or stark naked, you'd have me, Louise. I've known that from the first moment I saw you watching me back at the hotel. I've seen that look in a woman's eyes often enough to recognise it, so why deny it now? I might abhor your morals, just as you hate me for seeing through what you are, but neither of us can deny that there is a certain chemistry between us. Just don't make the mistake of thinking that you can use it to your advantage.'

He let her go, and Louise fell back against the seat and turned away to stare blankly out of the window through eyes misted with tears of rage. She hated him! Hated and despised everything he stood for. He was cold and ruthless and arrogant and ... and disturbingly attractive, awakening feelings inside her that she'd never experienced before!

She groaned silently, ruing a malicious fate. Why did she have to come halfway across the world to find a man who made her knees feel like butter and her blood burn like liquid fire? And why in the name of all the saints did it have to be him, the most cold-hearted, infuriating man any woman could have the misfortune to meet? It really wasn't fair!

* * *

The huge ceiling fans hummed lazily, stirring the warmly scented air. Louise rested her head against the cushions on the rattan chair and watched the hypnotically rotating blades. She felt so tired, as though half a lifetime had passed since that morning when she'd woken to find herself in Wyatt Lord's bedroom. Was it really only a matter of hours? It was hard to believe it when so much had happened.

'Are you feeling all right, darling?'

The softly voiced question echoed with concern, but Louise wasn't fool enough to be taken in by it. Since they'd arrived at the house on Paradise Island Wyatt had acted the part of the loving fiancé, but now Louise couldn't bear to go along with the pretence a moment longer.

She turned to glare at him, her eyes filled with loathing as they skimmed his handsome face, the strong lines of his body. Dressed in a deep blue shirt and white trousers, with his dark hair lying smoothly against his well-shaped head, his tanned skin gleaming with health and vitality, he looked far more handsome than any man had a right to look. She had taken pains with her own appearance before she'd come down to dinner, dressing in a soft peach voile dress that enhanced the creamy gold of her skin and clung enticingly to the soft curves of her body. To the rest of the group gathered to dine at the Hutton home they must look like the perfect couple on the surface, and for some reason the thought stung.

'I'm fine. And you don't have to keep up the act all the time, *darling*. No one can hear you right now, so why not give us both a rest?'

He smiled tenderly, but there was no hint of tenderness in his cold blue eyes as he crouched down beside her chair and stared directly into her face. 'Perhaps nobody can hear, Louise, my sweet, but that doesn't mean that they aren't watching us.' He shot a glance over his shoulder, raising his wine glass in a silent salute as he caught his host's eye. He turned his attention back to Louise, his voice dropping a fraction, hard and cutting now. 'I thought I made myself very plain before about how I wanted this playing, yet so far you've done very little to convince Carling or her father that we are in love. I suggest you put a bit more enthusiasm into the act if you hope to earn your fee.'

Louise stiffened, her eyes murderous as they met his. 'Enthusiasm? How can I be enthusiastic about being blackmailed?'

He stood up slowly, one dark brow arching as he continued to watch her. 'I have no idea, but I'm sure you've had enough practice feigning "enthusiasm" over the years for it not to be too difficult a task.'

'If you mean what I think you mean, then frankly, Wyatt——'

'Not interrupting anything, am I?' Lawrence Hutton broke in on her tirade, his eyes curious as they moved from Wyatt to Louise's angry face. 'Don't tell me that you two love-birds are quarrelling.'

Wyatt laughed deeply, settling his glass down to take Louise's hand and raise it to his lips. 'Not really. I think Louise is just worried that I might be trying to overdo things as I wasn't well last night. I keep telling her that I'm fine now, but...' He

shrugged, linking his long fingers with hers in a
tender little gesture that effectively stopped her from
drawing her hand away. 'One of Louise's most en-
dearing traits is her caring attitude towards others.
It's the reason why I was so...' He paused deliberately, watching the way her mouth thinned with obvious displeasure, then carried on in a deeply husky
tone that set her teeth on edge, 'Well, so attracted
to her, in fact.'

Oh, if she were a man she would hit him! How
dared he do that, kiss her hand then mock her that
way by twisting the facts to suit his own purposes?
Louise curled her fingers, digging her nails into the
palm of his hand, hearing his soft indrawn breath
of pain.

'I can sure understand that. There is nothing quite
as attractive in a woman as compassion and caring.'
Lawrence Hutton smiled warmly down at Louise.
'My wife was blessed with those very same qual-
ities, in fact.' He glanced across the room, his face
aglow with fatherly pride. 'Carling is just like her
in that respect, I'm delighted to say.'

Louise held back a snort of laughter, turning it
hastily into a cough. The last thing she'd call
Carling Hutton was caring and compassionate!
From the moment she'd met them at the airstrip
she'd made it plain, to Louise at least, that while
she might *care* to have Wyatt here she didn't *care*
to have Louise! There had been open hostility in
the younger woman's eyes every time they had focused on Louise, although she was careful to hide
it from her father and Wyatt.

'She's a lovely girl, Lawrence.' Wyatt let her hand
drop to pick up his glass again.

'She is indeed. Why, I had hoped that you...'
He stopped abruptly, a hint of discomfort in his
expression. 'Well, never mind that. I don't think
I've actually congratulated you yet, Wyatt, on your
engagement. I must say that I was surprised when
Carling told me; I had no idea it was on the cards.'

Was that just the faintest trace of disbelief in
Lawrence Hutton's voice? Obviously Wyatt Lord
thought so too, because his eyes narrowed a
fraction, although his voice sounded perfectly level
when he answered. 'I'm sure you didn't. There are
some things I prefer to keep quiet about, and this
was one of them.'

'I guess I can understand that. With your track
record, son, the Press will have a field-day once
this leaks out—as it will soon, I imagine. In fact
Carling was saying something about throwing a
party for you both to celebrate while you're here.'

Wyatt smiled calmly, but Louise could see a
sudden tension in his body as he glanced from his
host to her. 'That's kind of you, Lawrence, but I
think we'd both prefer it if we kept things quiet a
while longer. Don't you agree, darling?'

Was it the 'darling' that did it; the coldly mocking
use of the endearment that sounded more like an
order for her to follow his lead than anything else?
Louise had no way of knowing what it was that
suddenly annoyed her so much that she threw all
caution to the winds, intent only on paying him
back for everything he'd done and said.

'I don't mind, my love,' she said softly, sweetly.
'In fact I think it's a lovely idea.' She laughed
huskily, avoiding looking directly at him. 'I mean,

how many couples get to celebrate something as
momentous as this in such a perfect setting?'

'But what about your parents, honey? I thought
we'd agreed to keep this quiet until we'd had a
chance to fly back to see them.'

Was she the only one to hear the note of steel in
his deep voice, the only one who could feel it slicing
through the tension in the air? Louise glanced hurriedly at Lawrence Hutton, but he was smiling be-
nignly at them both, obviously oblivious to what
was going on, to this silent battle of wills that suddenly she was determined she was going to win.
Wyatt Lord had had things all his own way for far
too long!

'I know we did, but I'm sure they'll understand
if we send them a telegram.' She stood up slowly,
slipping her arm into Wyatt's to rest her head
against his shoulder in a loving little gesture.
'Darling, there couldn't be a more perfect place to
celebrate our love for one another than here in
Paradise, could there?'

'Of course there couldn't! Well, that's settled,
then. Good. I'll tell Carling.'

Lawrence bustled away across the room to where
his daughter was chatting to another couple, leaving
behind him a wake of silence. Slowly Louise raised
her head from its hard cushion, then felt a shiver
run through her when she saw the fury in Wyatt's
pale eyes. Without a word he caught her by the
arm, his fingers bruising as he all but pushed her
through the patio doors and along the veranda to
a spot where they wouldn't be overheard.

'Let me go, you bully! You're hurting me!' With
a sharp twist of her arm she freed herself, rubbing

her flesh to ease the numbing pain left by his fingers.

'I'll do more than that if you don't tell me what you're up to, lady. What the hell did you think you were doing just now?'

He took a threatening step towards her and Louise backed away, stopping when she came up against the ornate white rail that marked the edge of the veranda. She turned round, gripping it tightly as she strove to hang on to her control, but as he came up to stop behind her she could feel a shudder inch its way coldly down her spine.

'I asked you a question and I'm waiting for an answer.'

'I . . . I wasn't playing at anything,' she muttered.

'Come on! Don't give me that.' He caught her shoulder and spun her round to face him, his face all stark angles in the pale rays of moonlight, his eyes gleaming like silver. 'You're up to something, and I want to know what it is!'

'I'm not up to anything, apart from doing what you told me to do.' She smiled tightly, watching the way his eyes narrowed assessingly. 'You were the one who told me to make this pretence of ours seem more realistic, so you only have yourself to blame if I acted the part of the loving little fiancée rather too well for your liking. After all, darling, what could be more romantic than an engagement party in this tropical paradise?'

'I mentioned nothing about engagement parties.'

She shrugged, moving away from the rail to go back inside. 'Then you should have made it clear what you expected. You only have yourself to blame if I didn't understand what you meant.'

'I see. You're saying that I should have been more specific?'

'I... You could put it that way.' Suddenly her heart started to hammer fast, the blood spinning through her veins, making her feel giddy. Why was he watching her like that, his eyes holding hers before dropping with deliberation to her mouth?

Louise wet her parched lips, her whole body tensing as he reached out and traced a finger slowly across the dampness of her lower lip. She jerked her head away, clenching her hands to stop herself from rubbing her finger across her mouth. 'Stop that! I don't know what you think you're doing——'

'I imagine that's obvious.' He took a step forwards, backing her against the rail, pinning her there with the strength of his body as he once more trailed a lazy, disturbing finger around the soft swell of her mouth. 'You just told me that I should have been more specific about what I expected, so...' He shrugged carelessly, his fingers leaving her mouth to stroke softly across the smoothness of her cheek, pushing the silky curls aside while he outlined the delicate curve of her ear.

Louise drew in a shuddering breath, her whole body shaking with a mixture of emotions, but there was only one of them she could afford to concentrate on right now. Deliberately, she whipped up her anger, using it as a shield against all the other, far more disturbing feelings he was awakening.

'I know what I said! However, that doesn't mean that I need a demonstration. I'm sure my imagination can stretch to acting the role of loving fiancée, difficult though it may be!'

'I'm sure it can. I'm sure this won't be the first time that you've pretended to have feelings for a man, but this time it isn't just a case of duping some poor besotted fool. This time there's Carling and Lawrence to convince as well, and frankly I can't afford to have you make any mistakes.' With a speed that was startling, he reached out and hauled her into his arms, holding her so tightly that she could barely breathe as he stared mockingly down into her shocked face. 'Let's call this a rehearsal, shall we, honey?'

His mouth came down, taking hers in a bruising kiss before she had time to utter a word of protest, let alone reason. Louise moaned softly, frantically trying to turn her head away from the cruelly punishing kiss, but he wouldn't let her. His hand came up, his fingers lacing through the short dark curls as he tilted her head back to deepen the kiss, his tongue forcing its way inside her mouth with an insulting disregard for her wants. Tears gathered in her eyes and spilled over, trickling hotly down her cheeks into the corner of her mouth so that she could taste their saltiness against the soreness of her lips.

Suddenly he stilled, his head lifting as he stared down into her white face, watching the glittering trail of tears sliding silently down her cheeks. Slowly he ran a finger over the wetness on her cheek, his touch so gentle now that for some reason Louise cried all the harder, her slender body shuddering with sobs.

'Shhh.' His hands came up to frame her face, tilting it up so that he could look deep into her tear-

soaked eyes, a faint frown darkening his brow, as
though something puzzled him.

'Let me go, Wyatt, please. Don't do this.' Her
voice was a husky murmur, half choked with sobs.
She knew what he thought of her—he'd made that
plain from the first moment they had met—yet
somehow it hurt to have him treat her this way,
with such a total disregard for her feelings. If he
had shouted it aloud he couldn't have made it
clearer how much he despised her.

He shook his head, his hands still framing her
face, yet so gentle now that they cradled rather than
held. 'Not yet. Not until we've made this rehearsal
as successful as I intend it to be.'

She couldn't stand any more, couldn't stand to
have him kiss her again in that same insulting way.
'No! No, I won't let you do——'

His head came down, his mouth catching the
frantic protests, cutting them off at once. Louise
closed her eyes, feeling pain swamp her at the
thought of what was to come, but this time it was
different. This time there was no cruelty in the way
his mouth moulded itself to hers, no harshness in
the firm, warm pressure of his lips against hers. If
Wyatt meant to punish this time, then it was a different kind of punishment, a new way to torment.

When his mouth opened against hers and as his
tongue traced the curve of her upper lip Louise
shuddered. Slowly, delicately, he outlined her lips,
the touch so light that it was more dream-like than
real, more fantasy than fact. When he raised his
head a fraction she drew in a shaky little breath,
feeling the tingling imprint burning against the soft
skin of her lips.

'Open your mouth for me, honey,' he whispered softly, his voice deep and rich in the silence of the night. Louise stared up at him, her eyes huge, shocked, reflecting all her inner turmoil as she shook her head. He smiled gently, lowering his head to kiss her again, to repeat the tantalising tracing of her mouth with his tongue, his hand smoothing up and down her back as he felt a shudder ripple through her body at the sensations he was creating before once more he drew back and repeated the soft request.

'No.' Was that really her voice sounding so faint and shaky? Louise was as shocked by that as she was by the way her heart was pounding and her body aching. What was happening to her? How could Wyatt make her feel this way after what he had done?

The questions tumbled through her head, but there was no time to find answers to any of them, as once more he kissed her, softly, sweetly, drawing a moan from her lips. She was weakening now, she could tell, her body responding traitorously to each soft caress, each delicate touch. She had to stop this now before she gave in completely and he achieved his objective.

She pushed against his chest, her fingers spreading across the hard muscles as she tried to make him free her, but it was the biggest mistake she could have made when she was so vulnerable. The feel of his hair-roughened skin through the thin silk made her fingertips tingle, while the heat of his body seemed to flow through her hands, filling her with a fierce, hot longing she couldn't fight. With a tiny moan she slid her hands up his chest to curl around the back of his neck as she drew his head down, shuddering as she felt the brush of his moustache against her skin when she finally acceded to his request and opened her mouth for him, and everything spun out of control.

Each slow, delicious sweep of his tongue against hers was sheer magic, drawing her deeper and deeper under the spell he was casting. She was on fire, her whole body burning up with a passion she'd never known before, a passion she'd never experienced even in her wildest dreams. Nothing seemed to matter any longer; there was just her, Wyatt and this magic he was creating, and she never wanted it to end. She wanted to stay here in Wyatt's arms forever!

The thought cut into the haze of desire, bringing her back to her senses with a cruel speed. Louise dragged herself out of his arms and spun round to stare down at the inky waves lapping at the white sands below while she tried to get herself under control, but it was difficult when the roaring throb of the surf seemed to echo the pulsing of her blood, the warmth of the breeze to mirror the heat of her skin.

'Mmm, very successful, don't you agree, honey?' There was a thread of amusement in the deep voice that sent a chill through her whole body, and she shivered. She glanced round, then looked quickly away again, not proof against the picture he made standing there beside her, his dark hair mussed by the breeze, his mouth faintly swollen from the kisses they'd shared. She wanted to curl herself up into a tight little ball and hide away from the shame of

what she'd done, but there was no way he would
allow her to do that.

'Do I take it from your lack of response that you
weren't all that pleased with our...rehearsal, then?'
The mockery was open now, stinging cruelly. 'We
can always carry on and rehearse some more if
you'd like.'

'No!' She turned to glare at him, her eyes glittering in the dim light. 'I don't need to rehearse
anything, thank you very much, not now nor in the
future!'

He studied her in silence, then smiled as he
reached out to brush his knuckles across the swollen
fullness of her mouth. 'No, I don't think you do.
That was quite a performance you just gave, Louise.
I hadn't realised before what a good actress you
really are. You almost had me fooled, so it should
convince Carling and her father all right.'

He turned to walk back inside, leaving Louise
staring after him. Slowly she turned round and
stared blindly out across the bay, her hands gripping
the rail so hard that her knuckles gleamed bone-
white as she faced the fact that it had been no act.
Wyatt might have been kissing her to rehearse the
roles they were playing, but when she'd kissed him
back it had been for real!

CHAPTER FOUR

THE evening seemed endless. By the time Carling escorted the other couple to the door, Louise's nerves were raw from keeping up the pretence. When the younger woman came back, she stood up, avoiding Wyatt's eyes as she smiled at her host.

'It's been a lovely evening, Lawrence, but I hope you'll excuse me if I go up to bed now. I'm exhausted.'

'Of course, my dear. You go right on up. We want you to feel at home while you're here with us, don't we, Carling, honey?'

Carling smiled warmly at her father, but there was little trace of that warmth when she turned to Louise. 'Of course we do. You go right on up, Louise. An early night might do you good. You do look tired.'

Louise bit back the retort, refusing to give Carling the satisfaction of knowing she'd scored a point. She probably did look tired, and was it any wonder in the circumstances? Murmuring a brief good-night, she headed towards the door, then stopped reluctantly when Wyatt spoke.

'I'll see you to your room, darling.'

'No!' She forced a smile to take the sting out of the abrupt refusal, inwardly groaning as she saw how his mouth had thinned with displeasure. 'There's no need for you to cut short your evening, darling. I'll be fine. You stay and enjoy yourself.

You must have a dozen things you want to discuss with Lawrence.'

Carling laughed huskily, slipping her hand playfully through Wyatt's arm. 'Never mind talking business again. You and Daddy have done enough of that tonight. You promised you'd come for a walk with me along the beach—that's as long as Louise doesn't mind.' She glanced at Louise, triumph glittering in her eyes, before she lowered her lids with girlish coyness.

'Now Carling, honey, don't you think it——?'

Louise spoke up quickly, cutting off Lawrence's mild rebuke. 'Of course I don't mind!' She laughed softly as she skimmed an intimate little glance over Wyatt's set face, deliberately ignoring the warning glitter in his eyes. 'Wyatt is very fond of you, Carling. He told me that himself on the flight over here. Why, I believe he considers you to be almost a younger sister, in fact. So go along, enjoy your walk, and I'll see you all in the morning.'

She left the room, walking calmly up the curving staircase and along the wide balcony that ran the length of the hallway to her room before sagging back against the closed door with a heartfelt sigh of relief. She might have evened the score in that round, but she doubted if it was going to be so easy in the future. First there had been Wyatt and all his horrible comments to contend with, and now it seemed she'd have to spend the next few days with Carling adding her ten cents' worth! How had she ever got herself into this in the first place? Because pride had dictated that she shouldn't let Wyatt Lord get away with all those miserable accusations? She'd meant to teach him a lesson, but really and truly was it worth it?

She looked round the elegant room, her eyes skimming over the expensive antiques without really seeing any of them, as one thought surfaced through all the confusion in her brain: she had to leave. It was the only sensible course of action to take. There was no way she wanted to remain in this house, especially not after what had happened between her and Wyatt tonight, although she shied away from examining why that should be so important.

She ran to the cupboard and dragged out her case, cramming her belongings haphazardly inside with scant regard for any order. She felt as nervous as a cat now that she'd made her decision, but was it any wonder? She could only guess what Wyatt would do if he found out what she was planning. If she was going to carry this through, then she would have to do it tonight, not risk waiting until the morning and have him discover what she was up to. Wyatt Lord had some particularly effective ways of making his displeasure felt!

She was just snapping the locks shut when a knock came at the door. Biting back a tiny moan, she dragged the case off the bed and pushed it out of sight behind the bathroom door, grimacing as a second knock echoed sharply round the room.

'Just a minute,' she called breathlessly as she unzipped her dress and dragged on the pale blue robe. She knotted the belt at her waist, then went and opened the door, staring coldly at Wyatt, who was standing outside, one arm raised above his head as he leant casually against the frame. 'Yes?'

His brows twitched at the less than friendly greeting, but he made no comment. 'I just thought I'd check that you have everything you need.'

'Yes. Thank you. I'm fine. Goodnight.' She started to close the door, but he put his hand out to stop her, studying her face with narrowed eyes in a way that brought guilty colour into her cheeks.

'Why do I have the strangest feeling that you are up to something, my sweet?'

'I have no idea. It's your problem if you have an over-active imagination. And don't "my sweet" me. I'm not *your* anything!'

'Oh, I beg to disagree. While we're in this house you, Louise, are my fiancée, and don't you forget it.'

'How can I when you keep going to such lengths to remind me all the time?' She looked pointedly over his shoulder, a frosty smile on her lips. 'Where have you left Carling? You don't want to keep her waiting, do you? Not when she's looking forward to that walk you promised her.'

He laughed softly, moving a step closer so that he could stare intently down into her face. 'Not jealous, are you, honey?' He tilted her chin, studying her widened eyes. 'Mmm, I'd say they were grey, but for a minute there I wondered if they'd turned to green.'

Louise snatched her head away, glaring back at him. 'Don't flatter yourself, Lord! Carling can have you any time she chooses and any way, lock, stock and barrel——'

'Gift-wrapped...or naked?' He pushed the door, using his superior strength to open it wide enough to walk into the room. 'I think I get the message,

Louise. You don't need to labour the point, otherwise I'll imagine it's more a case of "the lady doth protest too much", if you understand what I mean.'

Oh, she did; she understood quite clearly and cursed herself for not playing things a bit cooler. The last thing she wanted was for him to start imagining she really was *interested* in him! That was far too dangerous.

She took a quick little breath, her hand tightening around the edge of the door. 'I won't bother dignifying that with a reply. I assume you did have a reason for coming here—other than a desire to annoy me, that is.'

'Do I, Louise?'

'Do you what?' She closed her eyes, then opened them again and stared angrily back at him. 'Look, Wyatt, you might not be tired, but I am. I didn't get much sleep last night and all I want to do now is climb into bed, not stand here talking in riddles!'

He walked over to the window, staring down the sweeping lawns to where the beach made a pale half-moon of light against the dark shadows of trees and shrubs. 'You didn't get much sleep because you were looking after me, isn't that right?'

She shrugged but didn't answer, watching warily. What was he up to now? What new game had he devised to torture her with? Yet when he glanced back across the room there was no harshness about his expression, just a faint curiosity in the pale aqua depths of his eyes.

'Why, Louise?' His voice was deep, smoky, stirring her senses by its very richness and beauty. A shiver rippled down her spine and she drew the robe tighter around her throat, startled to feel her pulse beating heavily as her fingers brushed the base of her neck.

'Wh-why what? Is this another of your riddles, Wyatt?' She'd wanted to sound firm and confident; it frightened her to hear herself sounding just the opposite—hesitant, disturbed.

He smiled slowly, moving away from the window to come back across the room and stop in front of her, so close that she could smell the faint tang of cologne and soap that clung to his skin, see the tiny pale lines that fanned out from the corners of those startlingly pale eyes. He looked big and indomitably male with that thick black moustache and the faint shadow of body hair she could see through the silk of his shirt. It made her feel strangely defenceless, incredibly feminine, her own smooth skin and soft curves a startling contrast to his hard body. Never had she been so achingly aware of the differences between a man and a woman as she was then.

'Why what?' She repeated the question, forcing the disquieting thoughts from her mind while she dealt with what was happening now.

''Why did you spend the night in my room, Louise? Why did you even bother to check to see how I was, quite apart from spending all that time making me comfortable?' His eyes gleamed as he saw the faint flush that ran up her cheeks. 'You *did* make me feel a lot better, honey. All that effort spent sponging me down was well worth it.'

'Then you've answered your own question.' She shrugged lightly, avoiding his gaze, all too aware of his nearness and the effect it was having on her pulse-rate. 'I did what I had to to make you comfortable. There's no mystery to it.'

'If it had been some other woman, then maybe not, but you, Louise...' He didn't finish the sentence, but then he didn't need to. She knew what he meant!

'Meaning that I don't usually do things without a very good reason?' She laughed harshly, hiding the pain behind a mask of amusement. It hurt so much to hear what he thought of her, even though she must have heard his view a dozen times by now. 'Don't worry yourself about it, Wyatt. I'll just add my charge to the bill. I wonder what the going rate is for nursing care over there? Not to worry; I'll make some enquiries and I promise not to charge you above the odds.'

His face froze, his eyes glacial now as they skimmed her face with contempt. 'Do that. I'd hate for you to come back to me at a later date with any further demands. We may as well ensure that you didn't waste the entire night!'

She hated him! Hated him for thinking such things about her, hated him for his pigheaded refusal to see the truth! Hated him for the way he could hurt her this way.

'Of course. Now if you've finished sorting out that bit of business...' She opened the door wider, wanting only for him to leave before she broke down and wept. 'Don't forget poor Carling, will you? She must be wondering where you've got to.'

'I'm not likely to forget her. However, both she and Lawrence would think it very strange if I didn't stop by your room to wish you a tender goodnight.'

'I imagine that Carling would be only too delighted if you didn't, but let's not go into that right now! If you've finished acting the loving fiancée would you mind leaving me in peace?'

'Of course not.' He glanced round the room, then let his gaze travel back to her face. 'You seem very on edge tonight, Louise. Is there something wrong?'

'No! Absolutely nothing. How could there be when I've just added a bonus to that ten thousand dollars you're paying me? Now will you please go?'

She sagged in relief when he finally stepped out into the corridor, then stiffened when he turned back. 'Before I forget, Lawrence asked me to tell you that the alarms will be switched on in about half an hour's time. So don't go wandering about the place or you'll set them off.'

'Alarms?' she queried faintly.

'Mmm. With all these antiques about the place, he doesn't believe in taking any chances. The house has a very sophisticated alarm system, which is switched on at night. But that shouldn't cause you any problems. Goodnight.'

He left at last and Louise shut the door then closed her eyes in despair. Great! That was just what she needed, the whole house rigged up to a system that would awaken the dead if she set a foot out of the door!

Wearily she walked over to the window and stared at the lights of Nassau gleaming across the bay, tantalising symbols of freedom, so near, yet so far away. She'd never be able to escape now. She'd have to stay here with Wyatt and put up with all his horrible comments. Unless . . . !

She glanced at her watch, her eyes bright with relief as she realised she didn't have to abandon all hope just yet. There was still time to put her plan into action if she left the house immediately. She could hide in the gardens until Wyatt and Carling got back from their walk, then set about making her way over to Nassau. If she could catch a flight out tonight then she could be away before anyone noticed that she was missing. She might have to leave her things behind, but it would be worth it. And there wouldn't be a single thing that Wyatt Lord could do about it!

The night was warm, the faint breeze blowing through the bushes where she was hiding tangy with the scent of the sea lapping at the white sands just yards away. Louise shifted slightly to ease her cramped legs, wondering irritably how much longer she would have to stay there. Wyatt and Carling had left the house a while ago to stroll down to the beach, then disappeared along a path leading towards the rear of the property. If this was Wyatt's idea of damping Carling's interest in him, this lengthy moonlit stroll, then he needed taking aside and talking to. A night like this was just meant for love!

For some reason the thought annoyed her intensely, and she straightened to stare round the deserted gardens. Were Wyatt and Carling still out here, or had they returned via some other route, leaving her hiding here wasting valuable time? With her luck and Wyatt Lord's track record, it seemed more than likely.

She glanced back at the house, her eyes narrowing on an upstairs window where a light was showing. If she wasn't mistaken, that was the room Wyatt was in. She'd been amused when she'd discovered that Carling had put them in rooms at opposite ends of the corridor—a not very subtle ploy to keep them apart. Now, as she watched, a figure appeared at the window, and she had no difficulty in recognising Wyatt. She stepped back into the shadows, then stopped when she realised that there was no way he could see her from this distance, not dressed in the black jeans and long-sleeved black T-shirt she'd chosen specially.

A smile teased the full curve of her mouth as she thought about how angry he would be in the morning when he found out that she'd gone. He would have his work cut out thinking up some plausible excuse to tell Carling and her father, but it served him right for being so...

Her brain turned to mush, all the sweet thoughts of revenge dissolving as a second, equally recognisable figure appeared at the window. Just *what* was Carling doing in his room?

The anger she felt was so swift and unexpected that Louise had taken several steps towards the house before she realised what she was doing. She sank back to the ground, forcing herself to get a grip on her emotions. It didn't matter what Carling was doing in Wyatt's room; it was none of her affair! He could entertain a whole army of beautiful women in his bedroom at any time he chose, and she was a fool to feel ... well, betrayed! She might have been brought here in the guise of fiancée, but she mustn't lose sight of the fact that it was all an act. Carling Hutton was welcome to him!

She stayed where she was until the light in the window was suddenly extinguished, plunging the house into darkness and her imagination into over-drive. Deliberately she blanked the thoughts from her mind and stood up, walking briskly towards the gates. What Wyatt and Carling were doing right now was their business. What *she* had to concen-trate on was getting into Nassau and catching that plane. Once she'd left the island, then she could put this whole unpleasant episode behind her.

She was nearly at the gates when something made her slow down. She glanced round, wondering what was making the strange flurry of unease ripple down her spine. In a slow sweep her eyes traced the shadows before coming to rest on two gleaming pinpoints of light by the edge of the path, and she frowned. What on earth were they?

The moon slid from behind a lacy black cloud, illuminating the gardens with a bright silvery light, and Louise bit back a gasp of shock as she saw the huge Dobermann pinscher dog standing by the bushes watching her. With its eyes gleaming red in the light and its mouth hanging open to display huge white fangs, it looked like a hound from hell, and Louise felt her blood curdle with fear.

With a tiny yelp she turned and fled back the way she'd come, expecting any moment to feel those vicious teeth ripping into her flesh. A sob welled into her throat as she scrambled up the veranda steps and tried the patio door, only to discover that it was locked. She shot a terrified glance over her shoulder and moaned when she saw the dog at the

bottom of the steps. It made a move towards her
and Louise gave a sharp cry of fear, then turned
and raced for the ornate iron staircase that led up
to the second-floor veranda, hurling herself through
the first set of French doors that opened under her
frantic hands.

She slammed them behind her and stood quite
still while she caught her breath, then gave a tiny
scream when a deep voice spoke almost in her ear.

'Well, this *is* a surprise! I never expected you to
come visiting me again tonight. And so eagerly, at
that. You must be keen, Louise. You almost threw
yourself into this room. What's the matter, sweetheart? Afraid that Carling might have beaten you
to it and claimed what's rightfully yours as my
fiancée?'

She must have done something *really* terrible,
committed some deed so awful that fate was determined to pay her back for such a misde-
meanour! First that hell-hound, and now this! She
opened her mouth to reply to the mocking comments, determined not to let him get away with such
an accusation, but he flicked a lamp on, bathing
the room in a softly golden light, and all ability to
answer fled abruptly. For a long, tense moment
Louise stood immobile, colour surging into her pale
cheeks as she studied the picture he made standing
there with just a towel wrapped around his lean
hips. Against the soft white terry cloth his skin was
coppery, smooth, making her fingers itch to touch
it and see if he was made of flesh and blood or
sculpted. No man had a right to be so perfect as
he was, a right to have such a handsome face and
such a perfect body. It made her ache deep inside

just to look at him, made feelings spring to life that she didn't fully comprehend.

'Well, cat got your tongue, then?' He moved a few steps closer, his mouth curling deliberately into a smile of cool amusement as he studied her flushed face. 'You know you only had to ask, Louise, and anything you desired would be yours.'

It was the way he said that, softly, seductively, that broke the spell. Louise straightened abruptly, pushing the tangled curls from her flushed cheeks as she glared into his mocking eyes. 'You have nothing I want, Wyatt Lord, apart from that money!'

If she'd intended to make him angry by the bold reply, then she failed miserably. He laughed deeply, moving so close that all she needed to do was stretch out a finger to feel the smoothness of that coppery skin and trace the hardness of those muscles. She swallowed hard, curling her hands into fists, refusing to give in to such a crazy urge, then felt her heart leap into her throat when he did just what she'd imagined doing—he reached out and touched her. Slowly the tip of his finger traced a path down her cheek to slide smoothly, tantalisingly on down the slender column of her neck to the delicate bones of her shoulder and linger just for a heartbeat before moving on, leaving behind a trail of fire.

'I . . .' She couldn't seem to get her thoughts into any sort of order, couldn't seem to concentrate on anything apart from the burning touch of his finger, but she had to try. 'Stop that,' she ordered shakily, reaching up to catch his hand with hers, then flushed wildly as she realised that instead of removing herself from danger she'd achieved just the opposite by bringing his hand into contact with the top curve of her breast.

She pushed his hand away from her, her eyes glittering with anger aimed more at herself than him as she glared back at him. 'Look, I don't know what you think you're playing at, Lord, but whatever it is forget it! I'm not interested! Understand?'

He shook his head, crossing his arms across his bare chest as he continued to study her in a way that made her shift uncomfortably. 'No, I'm afraid I don't understand. You come rushing into my room and now you claim that you don't want anything.' He shrugged, the heavy muscles in his shoulders moving in a way that made her breath catch and made the ache grow a fraction stronger. 'If you didn't come for the reason that springs first and foremost to mind, honey, then why did you come? It's rather late just to come visiting.'

What could she say? If she told him the truth about why she was here, then frankly she could only *guess* at what form his reaction would take. Yet if she didn't tell him, let him carry on thinking that she'd come to his room because . . . because . . .

Her mind went dead, shutting off the thought of exactly what he imagined she wanted. Louise took a quick breath, striving to keep the panic out of her voice. 'Look, this is just a mistake. I . . . I didn't realise this was your room.'

He went still, his whole body tensing, his face turning to granite as he stared back at her from eyes that looked like chips of ice. 'I see. I think I'm getting the picture now. I should have realised

that you would never do anything out of simple
desire, Louise.'

'I don't know what you mean.' Her voice
sounded whispery thin, almost afraid. It was the
way he was watching her now, his face set, his eyes
filled with contempt. It cut into her like a knife,
making her want to plead with him to stop whatever
he was thinking and hear the truth. But even as she
started to explain, he cut her off. 'Look, Wyatt, I
don't——'

'Don't bother. We both know what happened,
don't we? You mistook my room for Lawrence's.'

How could anyone sound so cold and contemptuous? Louise had no idea, just the certainty
that somehow she had to convince him that he was
wrong! 'No! I wasn't looking for Lawrence's room!
Why should I be?'

He laughed harshly. 'Do I really need to answer
that, my sweet little money-grabber? I realised how
taken with you Lawrence was tonight, but I just
didn't imagine that you would act on it so quickly.
I thought that you just might have the decency to
keep your grasping little hands off him, but that
goes to show how wrong even I can be about a
woman like you.'

The sound of her hand catching his cheek a
stinging blow was loud, so loud that it seemed to
echo round the room and fill her head with its
dreadful, sickening noise. For a moment Louise just
stared at him in utter horror, then turned and fled,
but he caught her before she'd gone more than a
couple of steps.

'Oh, no, you don't! You're not getting away with
that, you cheap little——!' His head came down,

cutting off the rest of what he'd been about to say as he took her mouth in a punishing kiss, but Louise could still imagine the name he'd been going to call her, hear it echoing relentlessly inside her head. A sob welled into her throat and she moaned. He hated her! He hated and despised everything he thought she stood for, yet he was wrong, so very wrong!

She pushed against his chest, uncaring that her nails dug into his bare flesh, as she fought to make some space between them and twisted her mouth free of the bruising assault. 'No! I wasn't going to his room! Stop it, Wyatt. How dare you do this to me?'

What was there in her voice that stopped him? Even hours later she still couldn't fully understand why he stilled. He raised his head and stared down into her white face, his hands still grasping her shoulders. A shudder ran through him as he took a huge breath, but apart from that there was no other sign of the anger she could sense that he was fighting. 'Then what were you doing? Why did you come rushing in here...?'

'As though all the hounds from hell were after me?' Hysteria rose all at once and she started to laugh. 'That's because they were! They were after me, or at least one of them was!'

The laughter rolled through the silence in the room, growing louder and louder until her whole body was shaking with it. Wyatt gripped her arms hard and shook her, but it didn't seem to help. It was all so funny, so very, very funny! Why couldn't he see that?

Her breath caught on a gasp and the laughter died abruptly as he brought his hand up and slapped her smartly across the cheek. For a moment Louise just stared at him in shock, then started to crumple as tears ran down her cheeks. He gathered her into his arms, cradling her close as he smoothed a hand down her back, his voice so tender that it made her cry all the harder as he soothed her with a string of meaningless words until gradually the sobs abated and she lay exhausted against him.

'All right now?' His hand was gentle as he lifted her face and stared down at her, and Louise nodded, feeling the lump in her throat thicken. How marvellous it would be to have him speak to her so tenderly all the time, to see that genuine concern in his eyes, but that was like wishing for the moon.

She drew back a fraction, rubbing her hands over her tear-streaked cheeks as she tried to find something to say, but there didn't seem anything left apart from the truth. It was up to him whether he believed her or not. 'I was trying to leave the house to get to Nassau and catch a plane back to Miami. I'd got almost to the gates when this huge guard dog suddenly appeared, a Dobermann if I'm not mistaken.' She shuddered suddenly, remembering her fear at seeing the animal.

'A guard dog?'

He sounded so surprised that she smiled faintly. 'Yes. Didn't anyone warn you about it? It's a good job that you didn't go wandering around, then, isn't it?'

He merely nodded, his eyes intent as he studied her. Louise turned away, all too conscious of the sight she must look. Why was nothing ever simple and straightforward about dealing with this man? Why did something always happen that made her appear in the worst light possible? And why did it matter so much to her what he thought?

'You saw this dog, then what happened? Did it attack you?'

He prompted her to carry on, and she pushed the strangely disquieting thoughts to the back of her mind. 'No, it didn't actually. It probably would have if I hadn't run back to the house.'

'Run? Don't you realise that was the worst thing you could have done? It's a wonder it didn't savage you!' There was a harsh note in his deep voice that brought her head round, and she glared angrily back at him.

'Well, it didn't! Sorry to disappoint you, Mr Lord. I'm sure you would have enjoyed that, wouldn't you? Seen it as my just deserts?' She laughed shrilly. 'I may as well finish this sorry little tale, I suppose, even though it doesn't end how you would like it to! I ran up the stairs and into the first room that I came to. It wasn't a question of me choosing your room, or looking for Lawrence's. It was a simple case of getting inside before that beast attacked me. And now, if you don't mind, I think I'll go back to my room before you start accusing me of anything else.' She started towards the door, stopping abruptly when he stepped in front of her to bar her path.

'Do you mind? I want to leave,' she said haughtily, but he merely smiled, hitching the towel around his hips in a way that instantly drew her attention to his near-naked body.

'I don't think so, honey. I think it would be better all round if you stayed here tonight.'

'Better? For whom?' She smiled to hide the sudden flare of awareness she felt, deliberately focusing her gaze on his face and away from the seductive attraction of his superb body. 'Don't tell me you're having second thoughts about what you want from me.'

'I imagine I'll have second and third and fourth before we're through. You're a beautiful woman and, despite everything I know about you, I can't help feeling a certain attraction to you. However, that wasn't what I meant.'

'It...it wasn't?' Her voice was husky. She swallowed hard to ease the dryness, feeling her blood pounding along her veins. He was attracted to her; it shouldn't have mattered a jot to hear him admit it, but it did...it most certainly did!

'No.' He paused for a moment, a strange expression on his face as he studied her. Louise had the strangest feeling that he was searching for an answer to something that bothered him before the mask of cool mockery slid back into place. 'Do you really think I'd be foolish enough to let you go and make another attempt to leave?' He stepped round her and turned the key in the lock, weighing it in his hand as he watched her expression change to one of shock. 'I'm afraid you'll have to spend the rest of the night here—just as a precaution, you understand.'

'But you can't do that! You can't keep me here.' There was desperation in the shrill assertion, but he merely raised an eyebrow.

'Oh, but I can, and I intend to.' He smiled slowly, walking across the room to the French windows, his hands resting lightly on the locks. 'Of course if you are really determined I suppose you could wait until I'm asleep then creep out of the window here. But then there's that dog to consider, isn't there? I wonder if he's still around.' He started to open the window, but Louise stopped him with a cry.

'No! Don't do that. You haven't seen the beast, but I have!' She wrung her hands together as she tried to find a way out of the mess, but there wasn't one. The door was locked and there was no way she was taking her chances outside with that dog. She was trapped.

'I'm glad you've decided to see sense.' He walked back across the room, his voice muffled as he disappeared into the bathroom. 'You choose which side you prefer. I don't mind.'

'Pardon?' She walked to the bathroom door, then stepped aside as he reappeared, dressed now in a pair of dark boxer shorts that sat low on his lean hips. In a fast sweep her eyes did an involuntary stock-take of his tall, muscular body before coming back to his face with an awareness in them she couldn't quite hide and which she knew at once he saw and understood.

He smiled slowly, arrogantly, his teeth gleaming white beneath the luxuriant thickness of his moustache, his eyes holding a glint of wicked amusement that made her heart give a helpless little flutter. 'I said that you can choose which side of the bed you prefer. It doesn't bother me.'

His voice had dropped to a husky rumble that vibrated along every sensitive nerve, stealing her

ability to think for a moment. 'Which side of...
What did you say?'

He flinched at her shocked screech, but held the
smile. 'I think you heard me, but if you'd like me
to repeat it——'

'No! I don't need anything repeating. There is
no way that I'm sharing any bed with you, Wyatt
Lord...no way that you'll ever persuade me to!'

He shrugged lightly, walking past her to toss back
the cover and turn down the sheet. 'Suit yourself.
Goodnight.'

He slid into bed, then reached over to switch off
the lamp, reluctance on his face when she called for
him to stop.

'Now just a minute. What do you think you're
doing?'

'I imagine that's obvious. I'm going to sleep.'

'But what about me?' She looked round the
room, taking stock of and immediately dismissing
the elegant but decidedly uncomfortable antique
chair that must have been placed in the room more
for effect than anything else. 'Where am I supposed to sleep?'

'That's up to you, isn't it? You're welcome to
half of this bed, but if that doesn't suit you then I
don't know what you're going to do.'

He switched the lamp off, plunging the room into
darkness. Louise bit her lip, trying to hang on to
what little was left of her composure. 'A *gentleman*
would have offered to let a lady have the bed.'

There was a lengthy pause and she shifted uneasily from one foot to the other, wondering if she'd
struck a chord, then felt herself go cold when he
replied softly with a wealth of meaning in his voice.

'If there had been a *lady* in this room, then I would have accorded her that courtesy.'

It was a long time later, when she heard the measured rhythm of his breathing as he fell asleep, that she let go of her control at last and wept.

CHAPTER FIVE

THE sun was just starting to rise, touching the dark sky with gold and vermilion. Louise stood huddled by the window, watching the shadows shifting and changing. She felt so tired, more tired than she'd felt in the whole of her life, as though every cell in her body ached with weariness. She'd give anything in the world right now to go to sleep, but...

She glanced over her shoulder, her eyes widening when she saw that Wyatt was awake and lying in the bed watching her. Hurriedly she turned back to the window, forcing herself to concentrate on following the trickles of colour seeping across the horizon, but there was no way she could pretend that she was oblivious to his presence in the room. When she heard the soft swish as he tossed the sheet back she jumped nervously, her whole body going rigid as he came up to stand behind her, so close that she could feel the heat of his body against her spine.

'This isn't achieving anything. All you're doing is making yourself exhausted, and for what reason? To convince me what a heel I am for not letting you have the bed?' He laughed softly, his warm breath stirring the curls at her nape, making her shiver with the unexpected intimacy. 'It will take more than that, honey.'

She drew herself up, forcing the bone-deep tiredness away as she glared at him over her

shoulder. 'I'm sure it will! Normal human emotions
are lost on the likes of you, Lord. You wouldn't
know the first thing about decency and compassion
and...' She floundered for a moment, her tired
brain almost unequal to this fresh confrontation,
then ended lamely, 'And chivalry!'

'Chivalry?' He paused, then continued softly,
mockery echoing in his deep voice, 'I should have
thought you were past the point of waiting for your
knight errant to come along on his white
charger... in both age and experience.'

'You know nothing at all about me, Wyatt!
Nothing!' She whirled to face him, grasping the wall
as her head spun with dizziness. In the dim half-
light her face was pale, her eyes luminous with fa-
tigue and a sudden anger she didn't want to feel
yet somehow couldn't control. 'You've built
this... this picture of me in your head, and that's
how it is. Nothing will change your mind about me,
will it? You're not interested in hearing the truth
at all, and why not? Because the great Wyatt Lord
is always right!'

'Not always, but I am right about the fact that
you're out on your feet and that it's ridiculous for
you to be acting like this.' With a speed that startled
her, he swung her up into his arms and carried her
over to drop her on the bed.

'What the...? Stop it! Stop it at once! I
won't——'

He laid his hand across her mouth, his eyes glittering dangerously as he glared into her shocked
face. 'Don't bother. If you're worried about your
virtue, Louise, then take it from me that it couldn't
be safer. Now for heaven's sake do us both a favour

and lie down and get some sleep for what is left of the night.'

The cold contempt in his tone stopped her protests dead. Louise rolled on to her side, huddling into a tight little ball as she felt the bed dip as he climbed in beside her and stretched his long legs under the cool sheets with a weary sigh. Obviously he blamed her for the night's fiasco, but it wasn't fair to do that! He'd started it by being so mean in what he'd said.

A sob welled into her throat, but she bit it back, then rammed her fist against her mouth when another one followed it. She wouldn't let him reduce her to tears again. She wouldn't give him that much satisfaction. He was the most horrible, pigheaded—

'For heaven's sake, woman, what is the matter with you now? Are you crying?'

He sounded more angry than concerned, and Louise gulped, rubbing a hand across her eyes as she muttered a muffled, 'No.'

'No?' He rolled over on to his side, raising himself on his elbow as he peered down at her and touched the glimmer of moisture on her cheek as he repeated the question in a tone that made her feel hot all over. 'No?'

'I ... No!'

'You're a rotten liar, Louise, a really bad one, and, believe me I've met a few in my time to make me a good judge.' He slid a hand beneath her head and deftly turned her towards him, studying her face with a faint smile on his hard mouth that seemed to knock the breath out of her body. What was so different about that smile? Why did it make her feel so shuddery deep inside, as though someone was stirring her emotions up, mixing the pain and anger she'd felt before with something hot and wonderful she didn't recognise?

In silence she studied his face, tracing the warmly mobile curve of his mouth, then bit back a gasp as she realised that was what was making the difference: warmth! It was the first time that he'd ever smiled at her without mockery, without coldness, and the effect was devastating. It sent an answering wave of heat down to the tips of her toes and up to the top of her head, a heat that seemed to consume every part of her as she stared into his face and almost drowned in the warmth.

'Louise? What is it?' He tilted her face towards the faint light filtering through the window, his pale eyes glittering as they met hers.

'Nothing.' Her voice was a whisper of sound, so faint that she wondered if he'd heard her as he continued to study her. Then slowly he slid his hand up her cheek, his long fingers tangling in the dark curls at the side of her head as he repeated the word and turned it into a question that somehow didn't need an answer. 'Nothing? No, you're right. There's nothing wrong at all.'

He was going to kiss her. She knew that as clearly as she knew that it was what she wanted, what she yearned for most in the whole wide world at that moment. It didn't seem to matter whether it was right or wrong, whether it was utter folly or made complete sense; it was going to happen. With a soft sigh, Louise tilted her face, feeling the soft brush of his moustache against her cheek as he skimmed a line of kisses over the smooth curve until his mouth found hers.

Softly, warmly, his lips took hers in the gentlest of kisses, which only served to make her ache for something more, and she murmured in frustration.

He raised his head, his hand still cupping her face, his eyes half shuttered as he studied her. 'What is it? What do you want, Louise?'

She didn't have the experience to handle this kind of intimacy, nor the courage to tell him that she wanted him to kiss her as he had on the veranda, hotly, seductively. She lowered her lashes, hiding her eyes from the searching scrutiny, and heard him laugh quietly.

'If you can't tell me what you want, then show me.' His hands slid down her body, skimming the soft curves in a way that made her tremble, before they closed around her wrists and lifted her hands to link them behind his head. 'Show me what you want, Louise.'

There was a moment when fear overcame her, a moment when her whole body seemed to freeze, then, as though they had a life of their own, her fingers curled into the thick dark hair at the back of his head, burrowing deep into the silky strands to press against his skull.

'Yes.' His voice was husky now, deep, stirring her senses so that she responded instinctively to the encouragement. Slowly, so slowly that it seemed as though it were part of a dream, she drew his head down and fitted her mouth to his, letting her tongue trace the firm, hard line of his upper lip before she drew back a fraction and ran a fingertip across the moist warmth she'd left behind.

'Don't stop now, honey,' he grated roughly as he caught her hand and bit gently at the tip of her finger, making her gasp at the swift surge of pleasure that shot through her.

He rolled on to his back, drawing her with him to press her hand flat against the warmth of his chest so that she could feel the doubly enticing sensation of smooth skin and abrasive hair against her fingertips. Unbidden, her hand started to explore, sliding across the hard muscles to curve around his ribs before moving down, tracing the enticing slopes of his body until she encountered the waistband of his shorts. Her hand stilled at once, her fingers lying curled against his waist for a second before she moved her hand back up to his chest.

'Surely you're not shy, are you, Louise?'

Was that amusement in his voice now? Louise stared into his face, but it was impossible to tell when all she could see was the pale glitter of his eyes, and then it didn't seem to matter as he drew her to him and took her mouth in a kiss that was everything she'd longed for and more.

When his hand slid under the hem of her T-shirt just as his tongue slid into her mouth to tangle sensuously with hers she moaned softly. A slow-running river of fire seemed to be flowing through her, the heat burning away any hesitations she might have felt about what she was doing. Each slow sweep of his broad hand against the silken skin of her back seemed to be echoed by the sweep of his tongue dancing with hers, making her yearn for an even closer contact.

Without even thinking what she was doing, she pressed herself against him, fitting her smaller frame against the hard contours of his, feeling the unmistakable hardness of his arousal with a fierce joy. He wanted her!

When he stiffened suddenly and seemed to be about to pull away from her she acted instinctively, pressing her open mouth to the strong column of his throat in tiny fleeting kisses as her hands stroked enticingly back and forth across his chest, her nails just grazing the smooth skin. He groaned deeply, his hands sliding round her body to cup her aching breasts as he slid his thumbs across the rigid peaks of her nipples, blatantly evident under the thin lace of her bra.

Louise gasped at the sudden rush of sensation he created, feeling the tug of desire growing low in the pit of her stomach as he caught the hem of her T-shirt and dragged it over her head, baring her to his gaze. There was a moment when even the world seemed to grow still as his eyes slid over her breasts in their lacy covering, then he murmured something harsh under his breath and lowered his head to catch one rigid nub between his teeth and tug it gently.

'Wyatt!' There was a helpless note of longing in her voice that half shocked her, half excited her, as she said his name in the silence of the room. What he was doing to her made her feel just a little crazy, out of control, yet more aware of herself than she'd felt before in the whole of her life. She could feel every tiny cell in her body coming vibrantly alive, tingling with the echoes from the sensations he was creating. It was as though she'd been asleep for years and now he was waking her to what it really meant to be a woman.

Tears misted her eyes as she drew his head away from her breast and bent to kiss him, wanting to let him know how she felt, that this was the most wonderful experience of her life.

'I'm glad you're not keeping on with the act, honey. It would have been a shame to miss this.'

His deep voice grated, sending an unexpected shiver through her, and she stilled, her mouth just inches away from his. 'What?'

He laughed deeply, sweeping his hands down to the curve of her hips before running his fingertips slowly and deliberately up again to stroke her nipples. 'I'm glad that you've decided to be honest for once. You want me, I want you, so why not let ourselves enjoy each other? It's not as though you're a complete innocent in this game. Obviously you know what's what, and thank heavens for that!'

How could she have been such a mindless fool as to allow desire to rule her head and make her forget why she was here? She pulled away from him abruptly and stood up, dragging the T-shirt down to cover herself, as she felt shame course through every vein in her body. Somehow she would have to learn to live with what she'd just done, learn to forgive herself for this dreadful mistake, but that must wait until later. Now she had to handle this . . . this mess with as much dignity as she could muster.

'Yes, I know what's what, Wyatt. I know enough not to let you use me.'

He rolled over and came to his feet in one swift, lithe movement that startled her and made her take a quick step back from the bed, but he made no attempt to close the gap between them. 'Use you?'

He shook his head, his black hair falling in silky disarray across his broad forehead, his pale eyes like steel. 'Let's not make this into something it isn't, Louise. I wasn't *using* you. You were with me every step of the way...way ahead of me at some points, in fact! So let's not start that, shall we?'

'I...I'm not starting anything. I'm finishing it here and now.' She tossed her head, to shake the curls back from her pale face, blinking back the tears. She wouldn't cry. She wouldn't let him know that it felt as though he'd just taken her heart and smashed it on the ground. She'd almost given herself to this man, willingly, joyfully, and it had in truth meant nothing more to him than a means to assuage an urge. What it had meant to her she didn't want to think about.

'Finishing it?' He crossed his arms across his broad chest as he smiled cuttingly at her. 'I wonder why you made that sudden decision. Until I foolishly thanked heaven for the fact that you knew the score you seemed to be quite happy with the way things were progressing. What changed your mind, sweet Louise? Did it suddenly sink into your head that I wasn't about to fall for your little ploy?' He tilted his head as he studied her. 'Or am I being obtuse here? Maybe *this* is the ploy. You've given out a taster and now you don't intend to give anything more until I come up with a good offer?' He laughed softly in a way that made Louise want to curl up and die. 'Sorry, honey, but if you're holding out for a better offer then you're going to be sadly disappointed. I don't spend good money on something I can have for free!'

How was it possible just to stand there and let someone rip you apart, limb from limb, without crying out in agony? Louise couldn't understand where she found the strength from, but somehow she did.

She shrugged, her face betraying nothing of the pain and shame she felt. 'Then it's your loss, I'd say.'

His eyes narrowed, but he said nothing until she tried to pass him. He caught her wrist, his fingers encircling the fragile bones as he drew her to a halt. 'You seem to be handling this with great aplomb. Has it happened to you before?'

She shook her head, smiling at the sheer irony of the question, an irony he must be unaware of. She'd never been in this position before because she'd never offered herself to any man as she'd just done to him. How he would laugh if she tried to tell him that!

'No, I can honestly say this is a first.' She glanced down at his hand, then back at him with as much coolness as she could muster, praying that he wouldn't feel the fast beat of her pulse, mute evidence that even now she wasn't immune to his touch, as she wanted to be. 'I think I'll go back to my room. There's no reason for me to stay here.'

'And what if I won't let you go back just yet?' He dropped his hand from her arm. 'Don't forget the door's still locked.'

She laughed bitterly, feeling the ache spreading throughout her body. 'Then I'll take my chances with the hound from hell.' She walked over to the window and opened it, unaware that the rose-tinted light from the rising sun was casting its glow across

HOW TO PLAY
SIX HUNDRED THOUSAND
BIG BUCKS
SIX HUNDRED THOUSAND
AND YOU COULD WIN THE
£600,000
PLUS JACKPOT!
YOUR *PERSONAL* GAME CARD INSIDE...
Mills & Boon

IT'S FUN! IT'S FREE!

BIG BUCKS

HOW TO PLAY

It's so easy... grab a coin, and go right to your BIG BUCKS game card. Scratch off silver squares in a STRAIGHT LINE (across, down, or diagonal) until 5 pound signs are revealed. BINGO!... Doing this makes you eligible for a chance to win £600,000 in lifetime income (£20,000 each year for 30 years)! Also scratch all 4 corners to reveal the pound signs. This entitles you to a chance to win the £30,000 Extra Bonus Prize! Void if more than 9 squares scratched off.

Your EXCLUSIVE PRIZE NUMBER is in the upper right corner of your game card. Return your game card and we'll activate your unique Prize Draw Number, so it's important that your name and address section is completed correctly. This will permit us to identify you and match you with any cash prize rightfully yours!

FREE BOOKS PLUS FREE GIFT!

At the same time you play your BIG BUCKS game card for BIG CASH PRIZES... scratch the Lucky Charm to receive FOUR FREE Mills & Boon romances, and a FREE GIFT, TOO! They're totally free, absolutely free with no obligation to buy anything!

These books have a cover price of £1.99 each. But THEY ARE TOTALLY FREE; even the postage and packing will be at our

expense! The Reader Service is not like some book clubs. You don't have to make any minimum number of purchases - not even one!

The fact is, thousands of readers look forward to receiving six of the best new romance novels, at least a month before they're available in the shops. They like the convenience of home delivery, and there is no extra charge for postage and packing.

Of course you may play BIG BUCKS for cash prizes alone by not scratching off your LUCKY CHARM, but why not get everything that we are offering and that you are entitled to? You'll be glad you did!

NO PURCHASE NECESSARY - MILLION DOLLAR SWEEPSTAKES (III)

To enter, follow the directions published. For eligibility, entries must be received by March 31st 1996. No liability is assumed for printing errors, lost, late or misdirected entries. Odds of winning are determined by the number of eligible entries distributed and received. The sweepstakes is open to residents of the U.S. (except Puerto Rico), Canada, Europe and Taiwan who are 18 years of age or over. All applicable laws and regulations apply. Sweepstakes offer void wherever prohibited by law. The sweepstakes is presented by Torstar Corp., its subsidiaries and affiliates, in conjunction with book, merchandise and/or product offerings. For a free copy of the official sweepstakes rules send a stamped addressed envelope to: Prize Draw 96 Rules, Harlequin Mills & Boon, P.O. Box 236, Croydon, Surrey, CR9 3RU.

993 HARLEQUIN ENTERPRISES LTD.

TWO WAYS TO WIN BIG BUCKS!

1. Uncover 5 £ signs in a row... BINGO! You're eligible to win the £600,000 PRIZE DRAW!

2. Uncover 5 £ signs in a row AND £ signs in all 4 corners... BINGO! You're eligible to win the £30,000 EXTRA BONUS PRIZE!

▶ **DETACH AND POST THIS CARD TODAY!** ▶

EXCLUSIVE PRIZE N⁰ 567390u

BIG BUCKS

		£		

HURRY!

The jackpot *must be claimed!*

LUCKY CHARM GAME!

Claim up to 4 FREE books AND a FREE Mystery Gift!

Scratch Here →

10A5R

YES! I have played my Big Bucks game card as instructed. Enter my Big Bucks Prize number in the £600,000 Prize Draw and enter me for the Extra Bonus Prize. When the winners are selected, tell me if I've won. If the Lucky Charm is scratched off, I will also receive everything revealed, as explained on the back and on the opposite page. *I am over 18 years of age.*

Ms /Mrs/Miss/Mr _____ BLOCK CAPITALS PLEASE

Address _____

_____

Postcode _____

You may be mailed with offers from other reputable companies as a result of this application. If you would prefer not to share in this opportunity please tick box. ☐

mps

Mills & Boon Reader Service
FREEPOST
P.O. Box 70
Croydon
Surrey
CR9 9EL

NO
STAMP
NEEDED

it to:- "Big Bucks" Prize Draw, Harlequin Mills & Boon, P.O. Box 70, Croydon, Surrey CR9 3JE - we'll assign a Prize Draw number to you. Limit - one entry per envelope.

her face, laying all her emotions bare. 'If it's a straight choice, Wyatt, between that dog and you, then I know which I prefer.'

She wrenched the doors open and stepped out on to the veranda, her whole body stiffening with shock as behind her Wyatt said quietly, 'I'm sorry, Louise.'

Sorry for what? There was a moment when she stopped to glance back at him, a moment when hope flowed so sweetly inside her, then she turned and ran with a half-muffled sob which she didn't care if he heard. 'Sorry' could mean so many different things to different people, and she doubted if it meant the same to him as it did to her. All he was sorry about was the fact that she'd come to her senses in time!

Well, she was sorry too, sorry for being such a fool, sorry for getting herself into this situation in the first place, sorry that one part of her would always ache to feel again the joy he'd made her feel in his arms. That seemed more than enough to be sorry about.

The sun was hot, biting into her bare skin. Louise rolled on to her stomach, checking her watch before pillowing her face on her arms. Another ten minutes and then she'd go inside and get showered and changed ready for lunch. Wyatt might have allowed her to skip breakfast, but there was no way he would let her get away with missing lunch, and she couldn't face the trouble it could cause. The fewer confrontations they had during the next few days until she could leave, the better, as far as she

could see. It was the only way she was going to
survive.

She closed her eyes, willing the tension to ease
from her weary body, but it was impossible to relax
as her brain re-ran through everything that had
happened in the bedroom in a series of vivid freeze-
frames: her mouth against Wyatt's throat, his hands
caressing her breasts before his dark head dipped...

She sat up abruptly, shading her eyes against the
glare as she stared white-faced down the beach to
where Carling and Wyatt were playing a lazy game
of catch with a huge, brightly coloured beach ball.
As the ball whizzed over his head he leapt to catch
it, his body stretching upwards, every perfectly
toned muscle rippling in the sun, and she felt her
breath catch traitorously. She wanted to hate him
for what he had done, yet it seemed so difficult to
do that. Was she really so weak that just the sight
of a handsome face and superb body could make
her forget how he had used her?

'Are you feeling all right, Louise? We missed you
at breakfast-time.'

Louise jumped, forcing a smile as Lawrence
Hutton sat down on the padded lounger next to her
towel. 'Yes, I'm fine. I...I just wasn't very hungry,
that's all.'

He smiled kindly at her, but there was an intent
gleam in his eyes that warned her he wouldn't be
easily fooled. 'Sure you're not annoyed about the
amount of attention Carling is giving Wyatt?' He
shrugged as he looked indulgently down the beach.
'Perhaps she is just the tiniest bit spoiled and used
to getting her own way, but this habit she has of
flirting with Wyatt is totally innocent.'

There wasn't an innocent bone in that girl's body, and no one but a doting father could have missed seeing that fact! Louise swallowed the spiky retort and kept her tone carefully neutral. 'I'm sure you're right.'

'Good. I'm glad you understand. This was a surprise for both of us, I'll admit, but I'm sure that Carling is just as pleased as I am about this engagement.' He bent forwards to pat her arm. 'I have to say that I'm more than delighted Wyatt has found you, Louise. You remind me so much of my dear wife. She was——'

'Not trying to steal my girl, are you, Lawrence?' The relief that Louise felt at the interruption to the awkward conversation was short-lived as she looked up and met Wyatt's cold stare. She could almost hear his brain ticking over as he studied the tableau they made, her sitting on the towel with Lawrence bending solicitously towards her. She glared back at him, but he did no more than raise a mocking brow as he dropped down next to her on the towel and took her hand, twining his fingers through hers in a loving gesture that angered her even more by being so blatantly false.

'If I were twenty years younger then you might have a fight on your hands, but...' Lawrence smiled as he stood up and sketched them a friendly wave before walking down the beach to speak to Carling.

'I warned you, Louise. I made it very plain that you would regret it if you started playing games while you're here.' The contempt in Wyatt's deep voice sent her temper spiralling, and she dragged her hand free.

'I am not playing games! Why do you always look for the worst in every situation?'

'Because experience has taught me that's what I usually find.' He caught her chin, turning her face to his. 'I've told you once and I shall tell you again that Lawrence Hutton is off your list. I don't give a damn who you set your sights on after we leave here, but while you're here you'll respect my wishes. Is that clear?'

'Oh, perfectly clear! In fact it couldn't be clearer. Now if you've quite finished giving out your orders I think I'll go inside and change for lunch. That is if you will allow me to do so? I mean, I haven't actually had permission as yet.'

His eyes narrowed, pinpoints of silver light that seemed to bore right into her. 'I'd watch my tongue if I were you, lady. It could get you into a whole load of trouble you wouldn't enjoy.'

'Like the trouble I found myself in this morning...in your room?' She smiled with bitter sweetness. 'Now that *is* something I want to avoid at all costs!' She shuddered delicately, letting her eyes travel the length of his superb body before coming back to his face. 'I think one taster of what you have to offer was enough, Lord. I'll pass on a second.'

'Will you indeed?' His voice had dropped to a low, throaty growl that made her tingle with sudden excitement. She tore her eyes away from him, licking her parched lips.

'Yes.'

'Are you sure, honey? Absolutely certain that you wouldn't like seconds?' Suddenly he pushed her back on the towel, looming over her as he stared into her face, keeping her trapped with the power of his big body as he ran a lazy finger down the straight bridge of her nose to stop just a fraction above her moist lips.

'Stop it, Wyatt! I... What about Carling and her father?'

He didn't even bother to glance over his shoulder, his eyes never leaving hers. 'Too far away to hear what we're saying. To them it must look like a tender little interlude between lovers, and that's what we almost were, Louise—lovers.'

Her face burned with shame, and she turned her head, but he was relentless as he turned it back and held it there.

'Why are you doing this? Why are you being so cruel, Wyatt?'

He stilled for a moment, as though something in her tone had bothered him, but then he shrugged. 'Is it cruel to make a person see the truth? You wanted to make love with me this morning, honey, just as much as I wanted it. Don't try lying about how you felt now.'

'I thought you'd changed your mind, realised it was all an act I'd put on to trap you!'

'I doubt anyone could have acted the part as well as you did. Oh, maybe there was some thought at the back of that scheming little mind about how to make the most of the desire we both felt, but you wanted it as much as I did.' His thumb brushed her mouth, easing the lower lip down to run over the soft inner flesh as he watched her face and smiled when he saw the tiny flicker of desire in her eyes. Desperately she strove for something to say, something to make him realise that he was wrong, but it was difficult to disguise the truth.

'Yet you still accuse me of trying to attract Lawrence's attention?' She laughed shrilly. 'That doesn't make any sense!'

He stared arrogantly back at her. 'To you Lawrence is a business proposition, a way to get your hands on some money. It's different with you and me, Louise.'

'Different? In which way?' She glared at him, hating him for his arrogance and for the way that he could make her feel.

'Because you can't separate your emotions quite so neatly with me. Your greed for money is almost equalled by the need you feel to have me make love with you.'

'No!' With a surge of strength she pushed him away and scrambled to her feet. 'The only reason why I'm here, Lord, is because you made me come! You blackmailed me into this trip in the first place and I foolishly thought that I'd go along with it just to teach you a lesson, but I'm fast coming to realise that it's not worth it! Frankly, as far as I'm concerned both you and your money can go to——'

'My, my, what have we here? Surely you two aren't quarrelling again?'

Carling's husky voice cut into her tirade, and Louise glanced over her shoulder, feeling colour swim into her face as she saw the other woman standing just behind her. With her blonde hair caught on top of her head in an elegant knot and her sleek golden limbs perfectly displayed by the emerald bikini, she looked like something from a fashion magazine, and just as false. That was the whole problem; they were all living this stupid lie: she acting as Wyatt's loving fiancée, Carling pretending to be the perfect hostess. It was about time that they all came clean.

'Yes, we were quarrelling, Carling. Would you like to know why? I think it's about time that you learned the truth, then maybe we can all put an end to this . . . this masquerade!'

She glanced down at Wyatt and felt her stomach roll as she saw the anger on his face. Deliberately she turned away, telling herself that there was nothing he could do to her, but at the back of her mind a small voice was whispering that he could. It made her hesitate for an instant, and he took advantage of it at once.

He rolled to his feet, smiling as though he hadn't a care in the world. 'You'll have to excuse Louise. She's annoyed because I played a trick on her.' He laughed as he looped an arm around Louise's rigid shoulders. 'I've tried to apologise, and of course it isn't the first time that someone has thought the dog was vicious. After all, Lawrence did originally buy him as a guard dog; he wasn't to know what an old softie he'd turn out to be.'

What on earth was he saying? Louise stared at him in confusion, then felt her heart somersault when he bent and brushed a lingering kiss on her lips. 'I really am sorry, darling. I should have told you that the dog was harmless, but it was such an opportunity to have you stay the night with me.' He shrugged attractively, smiling over her head at Carling, who was watching the exchange with a smile pasted to her mouth.

'Are you saying that Louise was scared by the dog?'

'Mmm.' He laughed easily. 'I'd better start at the beginning. Louise came downstairs to find us last night while we were out walking, but came across the dog instead. She'd no idea that he wasn't dangerous. In fact he scared the life out of her. She came rushing back to the house and into my room, and I very wickedly decided not to explain that he wouldn't hurt a fly, let alone touch her.' He laid a hand over his heart, wry apology etched on his handsome face. 'I'm sorry, my sweet. I shouldn't have done it, but it was too much of a temptation to resist. And you must admit that the results made it worthwhile.'

The deep note of intimacy brought the colour into her face, and she gasped, 'Oh, but it——'

'Now I understand. However, it would be better if you didn't wander around outside at night, Louise.' Carling's voice was sharp, her displeasure evident as she snatched up her towel. 'You were fortunate that you tried Wyatt's window to get back inside. I'd switched off the alarm in his room so that he could open it if he wanted to, but normally all doors and windows are linked up to the central system that goes straight through to the security firm which patrols most of the properties on the island. They can be a trifle trigger-happy if they think there's an intruder about.'

She said no more as she headed back to the house. Louise watched her go in stunned silence as she digested what had happened, then turned on Wyatt in fury. 'You knew that dog wouldn't attack me! Yet you let me carry on thinking that it would!'

'Guilty.' He bent and picked up his towel, draping it around his neck as he stared calmly back at her. 'I can't see what all the fuss is about. You heard what Carling said. Things could have turned out far worse than they did.'

'That doesn't excuse what you did! I could have . . . have . . .' She trailed off abruptly, all too conscious of the hardness of his expression.

'Waited until I was asleep and then left? Is that what you mean?' He stared back at her. 'Do you really think that I would be stupid enough to tell you that the dog wouldn't touch you and then be forced to spend the rest of the night standing guard? Of course not. The animal was a bigger deterrent than anything else could have been. Now I suggest we go back in and get changed for lunch.' He turned to go, then paused to glance back over his shoulder. 'And may I also suggest that you are extremely careful what you say to Carling in future. Don't be tempted to indulge in another outburst, or you will regret it. I never make idle threats, Louise. I've waited too long and worked too damned hard getting this deal together to let you ruin it. Whatever it takes, and no matter who gets hurt, I shall have those hotels!'

He moved away, but it was a long time before Louise summoned up the strength to follow him. She didn't doubt he meant what he said, and if it had only been those threats he'd made she had to contend with then she would have been sorely tempted to challenge him to do his worst and to hell with the consequences. But now there was something else she had to take into consideration before she did anything rash.

A shiver raced down her spine and she snatched up her things as she tried to suppress the fear. Embarrassment, unsavoury publicity, even the shock and outrage of her family, all those she could cope with because she'd know that they were all the result of a pack of lies. But if Wyatt ever chose to use the desire she felt for him against her then the damage he would inflict would be irreparable.

CHAPTER SIX

CONVERSATION flowed across the table. Louise tried her hardest to concentrate on what was being said, but it was difficult after what had just happened. She'd tried her best while she'd showered and changed to convince herself that it had just been some crazy flight of fancy that had made her so afraid, but as she glanced at Wyatt under her lashes she knew it was a lie.

Her hand shook as she picked up the glass of mineral water and took a sip, studying the way his dark hair lay so sleekly against his skull, how the ice-blue knit shirt strained against the powerful width of his shoulders and heightened the depth of his tan. There had to be some way to work out why he made her feel this way about him, but, so help her, it eluded her. She didn't *want* to feel this desire, didn't want to see the awareness of how she felt in his eyes, yet she couldn't seem to stop it. Somehow or other, Wyatt Lord seemed to have put her under his spell!

The glass clattered against the top of the white-painted iron table as she set it down, and she felt him glance at her, but she ignored the look. Picking up her napkin, she folded it neatly then laid it beside her plate.

'It worries me when I see you looking so on edge, Louise. Makes me wonder exactly what is going on inside that beautiful head right now.'

His voice was deliberately low, so that it wouldn't carry across the table to where Carling and Lawrence were sitting, and Louise pretended that she hadn't heard him. But she should have known he wouldn't give up. He reached across and touched her arm, his fingers closing over her flesh in a caressing gesture that didn't fool her one bit. She looked up then, forcing herself to meet his eyes, then found she couldn't hold the gaze and looked away, studying the contrast his dark skin made against the paler gold of hers.

'You aren't planning anything else, are you, my sweet? Nothing that would really annoy me?'

Threat rumbled in the deep tones, roughening the velvet, and she stirred uneasily, wishing she could stop the sensations that were springing to life as his hand moved slowly down her arm. 'No. I just want to get this over and done with as soon as possible. Don't worry, Wyatt, you'll get your precious hotels.'

His grip tightened fractionally at the bitterness in her voice, but he made no comment as he lifted his own glass and sipped the iced fruit juice. Tension hummed in the air between them, and across the table Carling raised her head, honing in on it, as she seemed so adept at doing.

'You two are looking grim. I hope I'm not wasting my time planning this party for you. You don't want me to cancel it, do you?'

'Carling, honey.' Lawrence smiled an admonishment, but his eyes were curious, and Louise sighed as she slipped back into the role she was finding it increasingly difficult to play.

'Of course not. We're looking forward to the party, aren't we, darling?' she said calmly as she glanced at Wyatt.

'Certainly.' He smiled back at her and just for a moment there seemed to be a genuine warmth in his expression, a feeling of a secret that only they shared. Louise drew in a shuddery breath, missing the rest of what was said until Wyatt spoke her name.

'Sorry?'

'I was just saying that you might like to help Carling with the arrangements while I'm gone.' He must have seen her lack of comprehension because he added lightly, 'Don't tell me that you've forgotten that I'm flying back to Miami this afternoon for a meeting.'

She hadn't forgotten because he hadn't told her, and why not? So that she'd have no chance to make any plans, of course! She stared coldly back at him, letting him know that she understood his game. 'I must have forgotten.'

'I guess it's this place. It does kind of have that effect on a person, relaxes you so much that you tend to forget what day of the week it is. Still, I might have expected that it wouldn't affect Wyatt that way. There's little that can take his mind off business—apart from you, Louise, of course,' Lawrence added with heavy gallantry.

'Oh, I doubt if it would be much of a contest if the chips were down,' Louise said sharply, then winced when Wyatt caught her hand, his fingers bruising as he hauled her to her feet.

'There definitely wouldn't.' He brushed a hard kiss across her mouth, then glanced at Lawrence.

'Louise would win hands down every time. Now if
you'll both excuse me I'll get off. Come with me,
honey, and see me off.'

He propelled her along the terrace, gripping her
hand so hard that her fingers started to go numb.

'You're hurting me. Let me go, you big bully!'
She twisted her hand, but he held on until they
rounded a corner and moved out of sight. He let
her go abruptly, his face like stone as he backed
her into the shade of some flowering bushes. 'I'll
do more than that if you aren't careful. I've warned
you, Louise. You either play this my way or take
the consequences, and you wouldn't enjoy them,
believe me.'

She went cold at the deep note of threat, but
faced him proudly, refusing to back down. 'I hate
you, Wyatt! You're cold and unfeeling and completely ruthless. You don't give a damn about other
people's feelings.'

'And you do?' He moved closer, but didn't touch
her, his eyes cold with contempt. 'Do you care
about all the people you hurt, Louise?'

It was almost laughable, if it hadn't hurt so much
to hear him say it that way; she spent her life helping
people, not hurting them. 'I don't hurt anyone.'

'No? Then what about the families of the men
you get your grasping little hands on?' He caught
her chin and forced her head up, his eyes glittering
now with fury. 'I wonder how many homes you've
destroyed, how many families you've split up, sweet
little Louise. You accuse me of being ruthless, but
it's you who are the truly ruthless one. I only take
what is rightfully mine!'

He let her go and turned on his heel, but Louise stopped him, incensed that he dared speak to her that way. 'You have no right to say that! You don't know a thing about me...not one thing. Everything is based on a pack of lies you've invented!'

'Lies? No way. Oh, I can understand that you're upset; it's hard to face the truth and admit what you really are, isn't it? You've probably convinced yourself that these little liaisons you have are all completely innocent. If the gentlemen involved choose to spend their money on you, then that's up to them, isn't it? But once all the money has gone then you move on, find someone else to keep you!' He laughed deeply, staring into her flushed face. 'You see, I know all there is to know about women like you, Louise—all I *want* to know, in fact. So save your breath, honey. I don't want to hear anything else. As long as you serve the purpose I require by being here, then that's all I'm interested in.'

'You're despicable, Lord...completely despicable!' She whipped up her anger, using it against the pain she could feel aching deep inside her, but he seemed as unmoved by that as he was by everything else. If she'd thought for a moment that he would believe her, then she would have told him exactly what she did, and why she'd been helping that man back in the hotel, but he didn't want to hear.

'I've been called worse things, so I don't think I'll lose too much sleep over it. Just one thing though, Louise... If you were contemplating taking advantage of my being away, don't bother. I took the precaution of removing your passport from

your room before. You won't get out of the islands
without it.'

'I hate you!' She spat the words at him, but he
didn't flinch.

'No more than I hate what you are.' With a speed
that shocked her, he drew her to him and kissed
her hard with a total lack of emotion that was an
insult in itself. Then he pushed her from him and
walked away without a backward glance.

Louise pressed a hand to her stinging lips, closing
her eyes against the sudden waves of despair. She
hated him! She did . . . she did! If she kept on repeating it, then maybe it would stop her from
feeling as though her heart was being slowly crushed
by each cruel word he said.

With Wyatt gone and Lawrence busy in his study,
Carling dropped all pretence of politeness. When
Louise sought her out to offer help with the arrangements, more out of a need to fill in the day
than to accede to Wyatt's wishes, she was almost
rude in her refusal.

'I really don't think that there is anything you
can do, Louise. It isn't as though you know any of
the people I need to contact, and I doubt if you've
handled this sort of a party before. Frankly, you'd
be more of a hindrance than a help.'

Louise hid her annoyance, biting back the sharp
retort. 'I expect you're right. It is kind of you to
go to so much trouble for us, though.'

'I'm afraid you're under a misapprehension;
I'm not doing this for you, Louise. I'm doing it
for Wyatt.'

'I understand that, but in the circumstances it is generous of you.' She paused deliberately, letting her words sink home before adding sweetly, 'It can't have been easy for you, Carling, to find out that Wyatt is engaged.'

Carling laughed, a faint colour burning in her cheeks, although her expression remained as frosty as ever. 'Don't get too confident! There's still plenty of time left for Wyatt to come to his senses before the wedding and realise what a mistake he's made.' She skimmed a look over Louise's rigid figure, her mouth curling into a faintly contemptuous smile. 'You do have a certain naïve charm that might have attracted him, but it won't last. That's blatantly obvious even now from the way the pair of you act. It puzzled me at first, that tension that surrounds you both, but then I realised that Wyatt is starting to have second thoughts.

'He's way out of your league, Louise, and some day soon he's going to admit that to himself. And when he does I shall be around. Now if you'll excuse me, there are still things that need to be done. I want this party to be perfect for you, Louise: one special memory to hold on to when this engagement of yours comes to an end.'

She strolled away and Louise slowly counted to ten, then re-counted when it had little effect on her anger. That woman was impossible! If it hadn't been for the fact that she knew just how Carling would gloat, then she would have gone after her right now and told her the truth—that she was welcome to Wyatt! Frankly, from what she could see they would make a perfect couple!

She was in the pool, trying to work off some of her frustrations, when Wyatt arrived back late that afternoon. She'd tried her hardest to put what Carling had said out of her mind, but as she saw him now, standing on the edge of the pool watching her, she could feel her temper starting to rise again. This was all his fault, every miserable minute of it. If he hadn't forced her to come here, then she could have enjoyed the rest of her holiday, even though it hadn't turned out the way she'd originally hoped. He had an awful lot to answer for!

'Either you're in training for the next Olympic squad or something has fired you up, honey. So which is it?'

She blinked water out of her eyes as she clung to the side of the pool, and glared up at him. 'Don't you "honey" me! For your information I've spent a miserable afternoon avoiding Carling rather than suffer any more of her nastiness, and frankly I've had it up to here! I suggest you stick around tomorrow, otherwise I'm throwing in the towel. It's bad enough having to put up with you, let alone have Miss Viper adding her tenpence worth!'

'Mmm, that sounds almost as though you've missed me. Have you?' His voice dropped an octave, dark and dangerous, and Louise turned her face away so that he couldn't see the sudden awareness in her eyes.

'No! Don't flatter yourself, Lord! The only thing I missed was your being here to sweeten Carling's nasty temper!'

He laughed softly, hunching down so that he could look directly into her face. 'Why do I get the impression that you're not being wholly truthful?'

He drew her head round so that he could study the
stormy depths of her eyes. 'It isn't a crime, Louise,
so don't be shy about admitting that you missed
me.'

'I did not miss you! Understand? As far as I'm
concerned you could disappear out of my life tomorrow and I wouldn't lose a wink of sleep.' She
backed away, forgetting where she was, and came
up spitting mouthfuls of water as she swam back
to the side and glared up at him. 'Now look what
you made me do. You're nothing but a menace,
Lord!'

'Typical irrational female logic. You blame me
for your mistakes.' He held his hand down to her,
laughter curling his mouth into a smile she *felt* to
the tips of her toes. 'Come on, let's have you out
of there before you drown . . . and blame me for it.'

It was just an impulse, that was all, a momentary
aberration stemming from all the frustration. In
normal circumstances she would never have done
such a thing. But then nothing about this whole
situation could be classed as normal.

She laid her hand into his then quickly braced
her feet against the poolside and pulled . . . hard!
There was a moment, one delicious split-second,
when she could *savour* the shock on his face as he
felt himself pitching forward, then he hit the water
with a noisy splash and disappeared beneath the
surface. Louise gave a tiny, half-horrified giggle,
then a small laugh which quickly escalated into a
peal of laughter that made her shake. He would be
so angry—furious more likely—but it was worth it.
He was so infuriatingly smug, so sure that he——

'So you want to play games, do you, sweetheart? Well, then, that's fine by me.'

The laughter curdled into a hard lump in her throat, and Louise spun round in alarm. 'I . . . You shouldn't have mocked me. It was your own fault, Wyatt. Wyatt!'

Her voice rose to a shriek as he caught her by the waist and lifted her high above his head then tossed her into the water. Louise struggled back to the surface, coughing and spitting water, then turned and started swimming for the side as she spotted him coming towards her again. 'No, Wyatt. Stop it!' Grimly she clung to the slippery rim of the pool, panting as she tried to suck in enough air to lever herself out of the water.

'But you started it, Louise. You were the one who wanted to play water games.' He swam up beside her, his dark hair slicked to his skull, his eyelashes spiky with water as he grinned wolfishly at her. 'Don't tell me you're giving up already. I thought you had more spunk than that.'

She glared back at him, kicking her legs to keep afloat, although he was tall enough to stand on the bottom. He should have looked ridiculous with his clothes still on, the blue shirt sticking to his muscular torso, the pale grey trousers swaying in the flow of water, but he looked less ridiculous than dangerous with that glitter in his eyes, and Louise felt a curl of excitement run down her spine, which she tried her hardest to suppress. 'It isn't a question of spunk! You don't play fair.'

He laughed deeply, a rumble of sound that sent an echoing tingle through her body. 'And you do? Dragging me in wasn't what I'd call fair. You saw your chance and took it. Fairness had nothing whatsoever to do with it, as it hasn't with a lot of things in life. It seems that you and I are alike in many ways.' He reached out to smooth a wet curl behind her ear, his fingers tracing the delicate curve before sliding slowly down the slender length of her throat to curl around her shoulder and draw her gently to him. 'I wonder if that's part of the reason why we are so attracted to one another.'

'No! Stop that, Wyatt.' His name was on her lips as he suddenly bent and took her mouth in a kiss that seemed too achingly gentle to be real. There was none of the harshness from before, no sense that he was trying to punish her this time. He kissed her slowly, tenderly, in a way that sent a surge of joy racing through her.

'Wyatt.' She repeated his name like a prayer as he raised his head and stared solemnly down at her, and saw him smile in understanding as he traced the soft, wet curve of her cheek.

'Yes, Louise?' His fingers were moving across her shoulder now, skimming so lightly yet so devastatingly along the fine bones, before they moved to the soft swell of her breast above the neck of her plain black swimsuit and stopped.

'I . . . I . . .' Deep down in some tiny place where common sense still had a hold, she knew she should stop what was happening now before it went too far, but somehow it seemed impossible to make that decision as he repeated her name in a way that seemed to have a strange kind of magic, a hint of promise that made her yearn for something that could never be. Tears filled her eyes and rolled down her cheeks as she stared helplessly back at him and whispered softly, 'Don't do this, Wyatt.'

'Don't do... what?' He moved closer, his thighs brushing hers as he closed the gap between them, steadying her body with his own against the pull of the water.

'Don't make me... want you.' Her voice was so low that it barely carried above the soft sigh of the breeze in the trees, but he must have heard her because he stilled at once, every muscle going rigid. Louise drew in a gulping, sobbing breath and stared down at the water, watching it swirling around her legs, gently moving her against him. She seemed to have lost all control over her emotions, seemed to be drifting back and forth, from side to side, like the water. What happened next was up to him; he held control over her destiny, as he'd held it since the first moment they'd met, she suddenly realised.

'Can I do that? Can I make you want me as much as I want you, Louise?' There was a harshness to his voice that brought her head up, and she gasped when she saw the naked desire glittering in his eyes. For a moment the whole world seemed to stand still, waiting upon her answer, and Wyatt seemed to sense it too. His jaw clenched, his hands moving up to her shoulders to hold her in front of him as he stared into her widened eyes. 'Tell me the truth, Louise. Tell me!'

She didn't want to tell him how she felt, didn't want finally to admit to herself that the desire she felt for this man went beyond the bounds of logic or reason. He had used her, treated her abominably, yet she still wanted him, so help her. 'I... I... Yes!'

His hands contracted, crushing her flesh until
she almost cried out with the pain he was unconsciously inflicting, then his head came down and
he took her mouth in a burning kiss that left no
room for thoughts of anything other than the desire
she could feel surging between them. His mouth
plundered hers, demanding a response she was both
eager and willing to give as all the pain and frustration welled up and found an outlet in this rawly
primitive passion that flared between them.

'Wyatt!' His name was beautiful on her lips now,
the most heady sound she'd ever heard, filling her
with a sense of joy. She repeated it again and again,
then repeated it silently inside her head as he kissed
her again with a drugging tenderness that made the
blood throb heavily through her veins. When his
tongue slid between her lips to tangle with hers she
moaned sharply, helplessly, and felt him still as
though in shock. He drew back from her, his pale
eyes glittering wildly, his face flushed as he stared
into her passion-drugged eyes.

'No. Don't stop. Please, Wyatt.' She was barely
conscious of what she was saying, her body aching,
on fire with desire for him.

He smiled gently at her, pressing a lingering kiss
to her eager, bruised lips before murmuring softly,
'I'm not going to stop.'

Swiftly he dragged the wet shirt over his head
then drew her to him again and slid the straps of
her swimsuit down her arms, baring her breasts to
his gaze for a moment before he pulled her against
him with a groan of agony. 'God, you're beautiful,
Louise. So damned beautiful!' The words seemed
to be wrenched from him, as though he didn't want

to say them aloud, and she stiffened as a faint fear
uncurled inside her.

'Wyatt, I don't think——'

'Don't think, honey. Just feel.' His breath whispered against her damp skin just a moment before
he kissed her again and all her fears melted away.
Each slow sweep of his tongue against hers seemed
to heal the pain and warm the coldness that had
lain like a lump in her heart. When he caught her
hands and pressed them to the sleekness of his chest
as he held her up in the water she moaned softly.
He was satin and velvet, his skin smooth from the
water, warm from the flow of blood beneath it, the
beat of his heart thumping under her fingertips in
a rhythm that nearly drove her wild.

She moved against him, letting her body float
against the hard strength of his, feeling the unmistakable pressure of his arousal surging against her.
When his hand slid up to cup her breast and stroke
the rigid nipple she trembled. Nothing had ever felt
like this before; no one had ever made her feel as
though her body were on fire and her soul had gone
to heaven. What was happening to her? Was it just
desire she felt, or something more?

Her eyes opened straight into his, wide, shocked,
filled with uncertainty, and she heard him curse
roughly. 'Don't, Louise! Don't look at me that way.'

'Which way?' She licked her parched lips, shuddering when she saw the way his eyes hungrily followed the movement of her tongue.

'As though you're afraid of me.' He crushed her
against him, her soft breasts flattening against the
rigid muscles of his chest, making her breath catch
at the deliciously disturbing sensations.

She shook her head, feeling the softly grating brush of his body hair against her nipples as she swayed weightlessly in the warm water. 'I'm not afraid of you in any physical sense. It's just that this is wrong, Wyatt. Wrong!'

She tried to draw away, but he held her fast, his arm locked around her waist as he raised her in the water and stared into her troubled face. 'How can you say it's wrong? It feels very right to me, Louise.'

His hands smoothed the skin at her waist, his fingers stroking across the soft curve of her hips before moving down to cup the fullness of her bottom and draw her closer. Louise gasped, fighting the pull of passion so that she could cling to the very last vestiges of common sense.

'No. Nothing about this whole situation is right! We've been play-acting, Wyatt. It isn't real . . . any of it!'

He bit at her lower lip, teasing, tormenting kisses that made her ache with a wild abandonment which it was hard to control. 'Is this acting, Louise? Is it pretend? No. What we're feeling now is very real, and perhaps that's the trouble. Maybe we need to face up to how we feel about each other.'

'I don't know what you mean.' Her voice was hoarse with desire, her body on fire with need of him, but she didn't protest when he reluctantly set her from him and drew the bodice of the costume back up with a rough sigh.

'I think you do, honey. I think if you're honest with yourself you'll admit that the only way to handle how we feel is by admitting to it. I want you; you want me. That's just a simple fact.'

'So what are you suggesting we do about it? Sleep together? Is that what this is all about?'

He smiled. 'It's tempting, isn't it? I'd be a liar if I said otherwise, but——'

'But what? No, don't bother. This is just another of your ploys, Lord, isn't it? Another attempt to get me into your bed and then blame me for it happening.' Her face was hot with colour and she turned away to lever herself out of the pool, but he stopped her with a gentle hand on her arm.

'No, it isn't. If it's anything, it's an attempt to understand what we're feeling. Desire is a strange emotion. It can stem from so many different things. We've spent every moment since we met fighting, and that can be a stimulation in itself.'

'So what do you suggest? That we call a truce and then see how we feel?' Her eyes were dark with confusion as they met the glittering brightness of his.

'That's just what I am suggesting.' He laughed softly at her gasp of astonishment. 'Why not, Louise? Why should this be such purgatory for us? Surely we're both adult enough to enjoy each other's company for these few days. Let's agree to end the hostilities, shall we?'

He had to be mad—stark raving mad—if he thought she'd agree to that! It was bad enough trying to cope when they were fighting, but imagine being subjected to the full force of the Wyatt Lord technique!

Her eyes flashed as she scrambled out of the water and glared down at him. 'No way! There is no way on God's sweet earth that I'm calling any truce with you!'

He levered himself out of the water and stood beside her, running a hand over his dripping hair to push it away from his face before staring back at her with an expression in his eyes that sent a shiver straight down her backbone. 'Then if there isn't to be a truce, honey, it must be warfare.' He skimmed a glance over her rigid figure, his eyes crinkling at the corners with silent laughter as they moved slowly back to her face. 'I must admit I can hardly wait for the battle to recommence. You make a very tempting enemy, Louise. Very tempting indeed.'

There had to be something she could say to squash him, some smart, witty little put-down that would wipe the smile off his arrogant face, but wasn't it typical that she couldn't think of it right then when she needed it most? With a haughty toss of her head Louise stalked away, trying her hardest to ignore the mocking sound of his laughter, but it seemed to echo inside her head hours later, a taunting reminder of everything he'd said. Truce or war...what a choice to have to make!

CHAPTER SEVEN

THE dress was perfect. Pale grey silk chiffon, lightly sprinkled with tiny white spots, it floated around her slender body like a cloud. She'd paid her cousin only a fraction of the cost its designer label merited and put it aside to wear for some special occasion. It had just never crossed her mind that that special time would be her engagement party.

Her hand shook as she smoothed the thin straps across her shoulders, and she turned away from the mirror, not wanting to see the anxiety lurking in the depths of her eyes. There was just tonight to get through, then one more day, then she could put all this behind her. She'd managed so far, so she'd manage now to convince the world that she and Wyatt were in love.

There was a strange heaviness in her heart as she walked back through to her bedroom, but she had no chance to examine the reasons for it as she saw Wyatt standing by the window. Dressed in a white dinner-jacket with black trousers and snowy-white shirt, he looked devastating, and Louise felt her heart start to thump rapidly. Since that strangely unsettling conversation they'd had at the pool she'd done her best to keep the atmosphere between them calm and even, somehow afraid that Wyatt would carry out his threats to start a war if she gave him half a chance. But it was impossible to quell the sudden tension she felt at the sight of him now.

'Haven't you heard of knocking?' she demanded sharply, but he merely smiled as he turned from the window to study her rigid figure in a way that made the blood flow a little faster along her veins.

'I did knock, but you mustn't have heard me. You look lovely, Louise.' There was genuine appreciation in his deep voice, and Louise felt a shudder of heat work its way slowly, devastatingly down to her toes before she got herself under control.

'Thank you. I thought I should make an effort to convince your friends that I'm the perfect mate for you, so I pulled out all the stops. I'm glad you think you're getting your money's worth.'

His eyes narrowed and he took a few slow steps towards her, stopping far too close for her liking as he studied her softly flushed face. 'I don't think we're going to put on a convincing act if you adopt that attitude, Louise. It's crucial that you both look and act the part of the loving fiancée tonight.'

She shrugged slightly, turning away to pick up the small grey leather bag which matched her slim-heeled grey sandals. 'Sorry, I do apologise. Looking the part is simple enough, but as for acting it . . .' She flicked him a perfunctory smile, her eyes shimmering with contempt as they met his. 'I'm afraid acting the part is becoming increasingly difficult, Wyatt, but I shall do my best, rest assured. Now if you're ready, shall we go?'

He shook his head, his face inscrutable as he stood in front of her, blocking her path to the door. 'Not just yet, not until we've ascertained that you really *are* going to try your hardest, my sweet.'

'Don't be ridiculous! Of course I am. Do you really think I've gone through all this to throw it all away now?' Her heart was going crazy, skipping and leaping inside her chest. It was the way he was watching her, his pale eyes studying her with an intensity that seemed to see right through to her innermost secret places.

'And that's supposed to reassure me, is it? Your word that you're going to do your best to pull this off?'

'Yes! What else do you want? A written guarantee?' She swung away, picked up the pad and pencil lying on the small ornate desk, and wrote in swift, bold strokes,

> I, Louise Carter, do solemnly promise that I shall try my hardest to convince everyone that I am madly in love with Wyatt Lord.

She ripped the sheet off the pad and thrust it at him, one delicate eyebrow rising in mocking query. 'Well, does that satisfy you?'

He read the note and laughed deeply as he crumpled it in his hand and tossed it towards the waste basket. 'I'm afraid not. I'd be happier with something a bit more...concrete than that.'

'What? Name it, Lord, then maybe we can get on with what we're supposed to be doing.'

'This.' He had her in his arms before she could think, his pale eyes glittering laughingly down into her shocked ones. 'I can't think of anything more convincing than to have you appear in front of all those people looking loved.'

'No!' Louise struggled frantically, but it was impossible to break free of his hold. 'How dare you? How dar——?'

He pressed a gentle finger to her mouth, his voice deeply mocking now, yet holding a note that made a shiver ripple in hot waves along her spine. 'All's fair in love and war, Louise. And we decided yesterday that it was going to be war, didn't we?'

'I didn't decide anything! It was you who made that crazy statement. You, not——'

The rest of her protests were swallowed up as he kissed her hard and thoroughly, his lips taking hers in a kiss of such devastating expertise that she felt her knees starting to buckle. Grimly she fought to keep control of her reeling senses, keeping her mouth pressed tightly shut against the persuasive pressure of his, but it was a struggle she knew she was destined to lose at any moment unless she managed to stop him. Twisting her head away, she buried her face against his shoulder to stop him from kissing her again, but he did no more than laugh softly as his lips moved to shower a trail of tormenting kisses down her cheek before he started to bite gently at the exposed lobe of her ear.

Louise shuddered, moaning helplessly as his mouth moved slowly on, the moist tip of his tongue trailing along the cord of her neck, leaving behind a trail of fire that seemed to inflame her senses to an unbearable degree. She shook her head, her voice husky as she whispered a soft plea for him to stop the torment. 'No...please, Wyatt...please!'

Deliberately he pretended to misunderstand what she wanted as he caught her chin and turned her face to stare into her eyes. 'Don't worry, sweet, I'm not going to stop.'

'I . . . No!' She pulled frantically away from him, but he merely laughed as he eased her back against the hardness of his body and bent to kiss her again, slowly and sweetly. Louise moaned in protest, curling her hands into fists against his chest, forcing herself to ignore the traitorous weakness that was turning her limbs to water. She wouldn't let him use her this way, wouldn't give him the satisfaction of kissing him back!

'Open your mouth for me, honey,' he ground out deeply, tilting her head back so that his glittering eyes met hers from the space of inches. 'You know it's what you want, what we both want!'

'No! Stop it at once, Wyatt——' The angry words stopped abruptly as he took advantage of the moment, his mouth firm and demanding when it settled against hers as he slid his tongue between her parted lips. Louise shuddered, fighting hard to quell the immediate surge of raw desire that shot through her at the intimacy, but it was impossible to fight against something her body seemed so eager for. With a muffled groan all the fight went out of her and she started to kiss him back, her tongue tangling with his in a rhythm that made the blood whirl inside her hotly and sweetly. Each sweep of his tongue seemed to wipe away more and more of her resistance until she was clinging to him, her body shivering with need.

When he suddenly raised his head and stared down at her she found that she couldn't look away, let alone hide all the emotions he'd unleashed inside her. For a long, tense moment he studied her

flushed face, the passion-filled depths of her soft
grey eyes, then slowly he set her from him and ran
a steady hand over his hair to smooth the
dishevelled strands back from his forehead. 'That's
better. You look far more how you should, Louise.
Now shall we go down and meet the others?'

His voice was flat, betraying nothing of the
passion they'd shared, and something inside her
curled up and died. It had all been a trick, a cruel
device to convince the waiting guests that this engagement of theirs was real.

Tears welled behind her lids, but she blinked them
away, refusing to let him see how hurt she felt. If
she lived to be a hundred, then she would never
forget this moment, never forget how cruel he had
been. 'I hate you, Lord. Do you understand that?
I hate you and I can't wait for the time when I can
pay you back for this!'

He stopped her as she stormed towards the door,
his touch strangely impersonal now as he studied
her turbulent expression. 'Hate me, or hate how I
make you feel? Isn't that the truth, Louise? For
once in your life someone has touched *real* emotions
inside you, and you can't handle it, can you?
You've pretended passion for so long now that it
must have come as a shock to find out what it's
really like.'

Her hand came up, arcing through the air, but
he caught her wrist, his fingers encircling the slender
bones as he brought her hand to his mouth and
kissed her knuckles slowly and deliberately.
'Temper, temper, my sweet. You don't want to ruin
all my good work, do you?' He pressed her fingers
against his cheek and held them there as he laughed

at her. 'That would mean my having to start again,
from the beginning, and, tempting though the idea
is, I doubt Carling would appreciate any further
delay to the start of her party. But if you find that
you want to continue this later, then be my guest.'
His eyes dropped deliberately to run slowly up the
slender curves of her body before coming back to
her face. 'In fact, if I'm honest, I must admit that
I'd welcome another chance to prove my point.'

Louise snatched her hand away, breathing deeply
as she tried to control the pain she could still feel
inside her. 'There won't be any more chances,
Wyatt. You've just had your last one. If you try
anything again, then I'm going straight to Carling
and telling her the truth!'

His anger was almost tangible, dark and scary.
'I would suggest you think long and hard before
doing that. I told you before, Louise, that I'll carry
out my threats, and I meant it.'

She didn't doubt it! So why didn't she listen to
her common sense and what it was trying to tell
her? Why did she quite deliberately carry on and
try to goad him! 'Maybe I'm not scared any longer.
Maybe I'd prefer those *threats* to what you did
just now!' She studied him with an insulting
thoroughness, enjoying the way a thin line of colour
settled along his cheekbones and his jaw tightened.
'Granted you know which buttons to push to get
the reaction you want, but that's as far as it goes.
You might be a whiz at business, Wyatt, but lovemaking...' She smiled slowly, trailing her hand
down his cheek and across the hard muscles of his
chest, and let it linger for a heartbeat before letting
it drop to her side with a little grimace of regret.

'Lovemaking requires more than the right sequence of moves to be wholly effective. I enjoyed the trailer, but I think I'll miss the full performance, thank you. Frankly, the thought of that is more off-putting than any threat you care to make!'

It took every scrap of strength she possessed to smile as she walked past him to the door. Deep inside a pain was growing, but ruthlessly she blanked it from her mind. She would never let him know how much he had hurt her just now. It would be a secret she would take with her when she left, one more bitter souvenir of paradise.

The noise was making her head ache.

Louise excused herself from the group of people and made her way across the room to where the patio doors stood open, sending a delicious draft of cool evening air into the hot, crowded room. Everyone had been very kind tonight, going out of their way to make her feel welcome, but that didn't help the feelings of guilt she felt at the way she was deceiving them. They had welcomed her as Wyatt's fiancée, but she wasn't really that. It was all a sham.

Unconsciously her eyes searched the room and found him standing next to Carling, chatting to one of the guests whose name Louise couldn't remember right then. What would it have felt like if this hadn't been a pretence, if this party had really been a celebration of their commitment to one another? She had no idea, just the deep certainty that it was something she would never find out.

He must have sensed her watching him somehow, because he looked up suddenly and his eyes met hers across the crowded room. Slowly all the noise

faded and Louise caught her breath at the sheer
force of the feeling that flowed between them. Time
seemed to stand still, the world shuddering to a stop,
then Carling claimed his attention and the moment
fled as he looked away.

A mist of tears clouded her eyes and Louise
turned to stumble through the open door, wanting
only to be by herself for a few minutes before her
control snapped and she did something she might
regret. It was cool outside in the garden and
blessedly quiet after the noise in the house, so she
made her way towards the beach. The sand caught
at the heels of her shoes and impatiently she kicked
them off and carried on towards the sea until she
could feel the coolness of the water on her bare
feet.

It was so peaceful here, the only sounds the soft
sigh of the breeze as it lifted her hair back from
her face, the slap of the waves as they unfurled on
to the white sand. If she closed her eyes and tried
very hard, then maybe she could pretend that this
had been some crazy dream and that she would
wake up soon back in Miami with only the worry
of how to spend the day to contend with.

She closed her eyes and let her mind drift in the
silence as she searched for the peace she so desperately needed, but it eluded her as behind her
closed lids an image started to form, the image of
a man with black hair and eyes the colour of moon-
touched sea water.

'Are you all right?' His voice was deep and quiet
in the silence, yet it seemed to fill her heart and her
head in a way that no other man's voice had ever
done. Slowly, so slowly that it seemed to demand

every scrap of her strength, she opened her eyes and turned to look at him, watching the way the moonlight silvered his dark hair and emphasised the strong bones of his face, and the image took on substance and became shockingly, alarmingly real.

With a murmur of wild panic she jumped back and heard him curse roughly as he caught her round the waist and steadied her as she stumbled. He drew her to him, his hands biting into her flesh as he glared down into her face. 'Don't do that, damn you! I'm not going to attack you, if that's what you're expecting.'

Colour flared into her face and she pushed against the hard wall of his chest, all too conscious of the powerful strength of his lean body and the effect it was even now having on her. 'Nobody said that you were! You just startled me, that's all. Now if you don't mind, I would appreciate it if you'd just let me go. I've had enough of your caveman tactics tonight to last me a lifetime, thank you.'

It was exactly the wrong thing to say, and she knew it the very instant she saw the way his face set. For a moment that bordered on eternity, he held her in front of him, and she could almost see the silent battle he was waging. Then with a careless shrug he let her go, pushing his hands deep into the pockets of his trousers as he turned to stare out to sea.

Louise took a shuddery little breath and shot a nervous look at him. He seemed unperturbed, yet she could sense a certain tension about the rigid set of his shoulders, the stiffness of his stance. If she didn't know better, then she would almost have im-

agined that she'd upset him with what she'd said,
but of course that couldn't be so. Nothing she could
say or do would dent his iron composure and
assurance!

'What were you doing out here?' His voice was
low, but she still jumped nervously, and she felt
rather than saw his jaw tighten. It was that more
than anything that made her hesitate, when what
she'd meant to do was go back inside. The last thing
she wanted was for him to think she was afraid.

'I just wanted to get away from all the noise...all
the people in there,' she answered softly. 'But you
don't need to stay. I'll be fine by myself.'

'I'm sure you will, but I'm in no great hurry to
go back inside.' He turned to look at her, his face
in shadow now. 'I'll stay and keep you company if
you don't mind.'

Louise laughed shortly, putting up a hand to push
the curls away from her face. 'Do I have a choice?
You'll do exactly as you want to, Wyatt.'

He said nothing for a moment, then suddenly
turned and started back up the beach towards the
house. Startled by such abrupt behaviour, Louise
watched until he'd almost reached the veranda then
suddenly heard herself calling his name. The wind
caught the sound and carried it out to sea, and she
felt a strange panic enfold her. She couldn't let him
go like this, didn't want him to go back inside and
leave her alone with just her thoughts. It was better
to have Wyatt here than spend time merely thinking
about him. 'Wait!'

She stumbled across the sand, stopping just a few
feet away from where he'd come to a reluctant halt,

feeling her heart pounding so hard that it seemed
to shake her whole body with its beat.

'What is it, Louise?' There was impatience in his
voice now, a rough edge that didn't quite hide some
other emotion which startled her so much that she
could barely think. To hear that note of regret in
Wyatt's voice was something she'd never thought
to hear.

'Don't go.' Unconsciously her voice softened, and
she felt a sudden fear at what she was doing. She'd
fought him since they'd met, used anger as a shield
against other far more disturbing emotions; to stop
fighting him now like this made her suddenly afraid.

'There isn't any point in my staying, Louise. I
didn't come out here to upset you, but I seem to
have succeeded anyway.' He laughed harshly, his
eyes skimming her set face. 'Do you think I enjoy
seeing you looking at me as though I scare you half
to death? I don't, and I wish to God that I'd never
started this in the first place!' He turned to leave,
but she stopped him with a hand on his arm.

'I don't want you to go, Wyatt. Not like this.'
She was shaking all over, a fine, tight tension
strumming along every nerve. What she was doing
was madness, yet she couldn't seem to stop now
that she had set herself on course. 'Yes-yesterday
you mentioned something about us calling a truce;
surely it isn't too late for us to do that, even if it's
only for the next few hours?'

'Why?' His eyes were cold and flat as he turned
back to her, his face expressionless. 'Why have you
suddenly changed your mind when yesterday that
was the last thing you'd agree to? Afraid you're

not going to get your money if you don't sweeten me a bit?'

'No!' The pain she felt at the cruel accusation nearly cut her in two, and she took a step backwards, staring at him in horror. 'How could you, Wyatt? How could you say such a thing?'

'Quite easily. I've several days' experience to base it on. I know how your scheming little mind works, Louise.'

He was relentless in his cruelty, and suddenly she couldn't take any more. With a broken sob she turned and fled back down to the beach, ignoring the angry sound of his voice calling her back. The waves slapped against her legs, soaking the hem of her dress, but she was barely aware of it as she ran on until her lungs burned and she could run no further. She sank down on to the sand, burying her face in her hands, and cried as though her heart was breaking.

'Stop it. You'll make yourself ill crying like that. Come on, pull yourself together.' His voice was deep and soft, his hands strangely gentle as he turned her to face him and smoothed the tousled hair back from her face. Louise closed her eyes, trying to hold back the tears she hated him to see, but they kept slipping from beneath her lids. With a low oath he knelt beside her on the sand and gathered her into his arms, cradling her as gently as a child, until gradually the sobs abated and she lay exhausted against him.

'Better now? Good.' He tilted her face, smiling faintly as she murmured and tried to turn away from the intent scrutiny. 'Don't worry, honey. You're beautiful even now, half drowned in tears.'

He ran a finger down her cheek and wiped away the last sparkling drops, then let his hand rest against the smooth curve of her jaw in a touch that made her pulse leap frantically.

Desperate to break the disturbing contact, she scrambled to her feet, avoiding his helping hand. 'I . . . I'm sorry. I don't know what came over me.'

He shrugged as he stood up and brushed the sand off his black trousers. 'We've all been under a strain recently. It's not surprising that you're more emotional than perhaps you normally are.'

'I suppose so.' She ran a shaking hand over her hot face, wondering if he was right. She *did* feel emotional, as though she were perched precariously on some sort of crazy see-saw, swinging first up, then down. She glanced at Wyatt, then looked away when she saw that he was still watching her, concentrating on brushing the sand from her dress, but it clung tenaciously to the delicate fabric. She must look a sight, and suddenly the thought of going back inside to face all the curious stares, not to mention Carling's scrutiny, was almost more than she could bear.

'How do you feel now? Do you think you can cope if we go back inside, or do you need a bit more time to get yourself together?'

His consideration warmed her for a moment, until it suddenly dawned on her that he was less concerned about her than with keeping up appearances. If she couldn't look and act the part required of her, then it could have disastrous consequences. Lawrence Hutton wouldn't take kindly to finding out that he'd been tricked!

It was just what she needed to stiffen her resolve.
She stared coldly back at him. 'Don't worry, Wyatt,
I won't let you down. I always give good value for
money, and with such a generous fee at stake I'll
do my utmost to see this through to the end, bitter
though it may be.'

He swore softly, viciously. 'Dammit, woman, that
wasn't what I meant!'

'No? Don't tell me you were actually concerned
about my welfare.' She laughed hollowly. 'No, don't
bother, Wyatt. I wouldn't believe you even if you
swore an oath on a stack of bibles! Now if you'll
just give me a few minutes I'll go and repair some
of this damage. We don't want Carling and
Lawrence becoming suspicious, do we?'

He caught her arm roughly. 'One of these days
you're going to push me too far, honey!'

Her heart was hammering, but she refused to
back down even in the face of his anger. 'One of
these days? We only have one left after tonight,
Wyatt, and I don't think you're going to risk everything just to get even with me.'

She shook his hand off and started back to the
house, slowing when behind her Wyatt said softly,
'I'm tempted, Louise, very tempted.'

Her heart turned over, but she carried on
walking, refusing even to look back at him. She
could cope with anything—Carling, Lawrence and
all their guests, even a den full of hungry lions, if
she had to. Anything but the threat she could hear
echoing in his voice!

CHAPTER EIGHT

'LADIES and gentlemen, a toast...to Louise and Wyatt and a future filled with happiness and love.'

The toast was taken up by the rest of the guests, glasses chinked, and Louise smiled until her face ached with the effort it cost her. Beside her, Wyatt lifted two glasses of champagne off a tray and handed her one, bending so that he could look directly into her eyes as he said softly, 'To us, Louise. May the future bring us both what we want most.'

Louise clinked her glass against his, her heart aching as she smiled into his handsome face. 'And for you that means the hotels, of course. So here's to you, Wyatt; may all your plans reach fruition!'

His eyes narrowed at the sting in her voice, but he merely smiled as he took a sip of the wine, then lifted the glass from her hand and set it down with his again on the tray. In the background the band had started to play a slow waltz, the soft strains filling the suddenly quiet room. Louise glanced round, then felt her heart leap when Wyatt caught her hand and led her towards the centre of the floor to the accompaniment of applause.

'I don't want to dance!' she hissed at him under her breath, but he ignored her as he drew her into his arms and held her close as he led her across the floor. Louise glared up at him through her lashes, holding herself stiff and unbending as he turned her expertly and drew her just a fraction closer.

139

'Do you mind? I can hardly breathe.'

He glanced down at her, mockery making his eyes sparkle like burnished silver as he saw the mutinous curve of her soft mouth. 'I didn't realise I had that much of an effect on you, sweetheart.'

'I'm breathless because you've got my ribs crushed in a bear-hug! So don't kid yourself that it's your devastating charm!'

He laughed softly, brushing a light kiss against the soft curls at her temple as he eased a fraction more space between their bodies. 'I'd hate to damage such pretty packaging. How is that? Better?'

It wasn't better; if anything it was worse, because now she could feel every inch of his hard body just brushing against her in a way that was sheer torture. She ground her teeth, refusing to let him know how much the light contact disturbed her. When he guided her into a complicated turn and his chest brushed against her breasts, making her nipples harden under the thin silk of her dress, she almost weakened enough to ask him to let her go, but some in-built strength carried her through the moment.

'It wouldn't be a crime if you let yourself enjoy this, Louise. No one would accuse you of fraternising with the enemy.'

'I am not enjoying it! So why should I pretend? I don't want to dance with you, Wyatt. Understand?'

'Mmm, I understand perfectly,' he replied softly, staring straight into her stormy eyes. 'But I doubt if Lawrence's guests would.' He glanced over her shoulder, nodding to another couple who had

joined them on the floor. 'I imagine they would
consider it very strange if we didn't dance together.
So try to remember that you're here to play a part,
will you? It seems to keep on slipping your mind.'

Louise looked away, hating the fact that he knew
exactly how she was feeling, how his nearness was
affecting her. That was the whole trouble: try as
she might, she couldn't control the awareness she
always felt. She took a tiny steadying breath as she
glanced round the room, then felt herself go cold
when she saw that Carling was watching them
closely, a strange expression on her beautiful face.
Hurriedly she looked back at Wyatt, smiling up at
him with as much adoration as she could possibly
muster. 'I shall do my best. We don't want anyone
becoming suspicious, I suppose. Not if it means it
could jeopardise our deal.'

His fingers dug into her back, warm and hard
against her bare skin above the low neckline of her
dress. 'Let's not overdo things.' He glanced past
her, smiling at Carling as they glided past her, their
footsteps matching perfectly to the slow rhythm.
He waited until they had danced to the far end of
the room, then bent a fraction closer, so that Louise
could feel his breath, warm against her cheek.

'Carling is nobody's fool, so be careful, Louise.'

Louise arched a brow at him, her grey eyes filled
with mockery. 'I'm sure she isn't. In fact if I were
in the business of choosing the perfect mate for you,
Wyatt, I would place dear Carling at number one
on the list. What I can't understand is why you have
gone to such lengths to keep her out of your life.
I mean, quite apart from the fact that I'm sure you
could have negotiated a substantial discount if

Carling had come as part of the deal, what have you got against her? She's rich, beautiful and obviously fits into the society you move in. What more could any man ask?'

'What is this, honey? Some sort of a sales pitch? Has Carling asked you to put her case forward, or have you decided to do it all of your own accord?' He spun her round, pressing her close as they slowed to avoid another couple who had come up alongside them.

Louise smiled up at him, amusement glittering in her eyes. 'It's an idea. I should have thought of that, shouldn't I? I could have charged her a fee as well, made this doubly profitable.' She laughed softly, enjoying the way his mouth thinned with annoyance. 'No, don't worry, Wyatt. I don't intend to do that. As for a sales pitch, well... It just seems to me very strange that you haven't jumped at the opportunity the situation presents.'

'Maybe that's because I don't see it as an opportunity, but rather as a drawback. Carling is everything you say she is, but she is also spoilt and wilful, the sort of woman who wants a man to dance attendance on her all the time.' He flicked a glance across the room, his face set as he studied the blonde-haired woman. 'Frankly, Louise, I'm not in the market for that. I'm not interested in that kind of relationship at all. I'm too used to living my life the way I want to live it to want to accommodate other people's whims.'

'That sounds very selfish to me.'

'Perhaps it does.' He looked down at her, his eyes pale in the golden glow from the chandeliers. 'But I learned a long time ago that a man has to be single-minded to achieve what he wants to in this life. There isn't room to consider other people's wishes.'

'And in this case you want the hotels.'

'Yes.'

She stared up at him with curiosity. 'Why do I have the funniest feeling that there's more to this than merely a business deal?'

'Possibly because there is. These particular hotels once belonged to my family. I want them back. It's as simple as that.'

'They belonged to you?' Surprise echoed in her voice as she slowed almost to a stop. Wyatt murmured something rough under his breath, then drew her to the edge of the floor, his expression guarded now.

'Yes. They were sold about fifteen years ago. I've been trying to get them back for some time now, ever since I was in a position to negotiate for them.'

'But if they are so important to you, why sell them in the first place?' She frowned suddenly. 'But you couldn't have sold them, of course. Not fifteen years ago. You would have been only... what... seventeen... eighteen?'

'Good guess. I was eighteen at the time, and you're right: I didn't sell them. I would never have sold them. My father did. I am merely rectifying the mistake he made.'

His voice was so cold and flat that Louise shivered in reaction. She studied his face, searching for some clue to what had put that note in his voice, but there was nothing she could tell from the blandness of his expression.

'And how does he feel about what you're doing?' she asked quietly.

'My father is dead. I make the decisions now. I don't answer to anyone. Now shall we carry on dancing?'

He started to lead her back on to the floor, but Louise slipped out of his hold. She didn't want to dance, now more than ever. What Wyatt had just told her bothered her, although she couldn't have explained exactly why. Avoiding his hard-eyed stare, she walked away, heading towards the buffet tables that had been set at the far end of the room. Picking up a plate, she filled it with delicacies she doubted if she'd be able to eat. It was just an excuse to stop him from insisting that they carry on dancing.

'Sure you've got enough?' His eyes skimmed the loaded plate before lifting to hers with cold sarcasm in their pale depths, and Louise felt colour steal under her skin as she realised he knew exactly why she'd suddenly discovered such an appetite. Defiantly, she chose a tiny puff of whisper-light pastry filled with prawns and a soft cream cheese and bit into it, pretending that she was enjoying the rich delicacy. Wyatt watched her in silence, leaning back against the edge of the table, his arms folded across his broad chest. When she finished the pastry and hesitated he raised a mocking brow. 'Don't tell me you've had enough already.'

Louise glared up at him and chose at random, biting into a fresh cream fruit tart, feeling her stomach churn at the sweetness of the confection. She chewed and swallowed every crumb, then set down the plate, knowing that she couldn't eat anything else without running the risk of being sick.

'You've got cream on your lip.'

Wyatt's voice was completely bland as he made the quiet observation, but she still felt a rush of colour stain her cheeks. Hurriedly she ran the tip of a finger across her mouth, then glanced back at him. 'Is that better?'

He shook his head, bending towards her as he caught her chin and tipped her face up to his. Louise stilled, waiting for the touch of his finger, then felt shock course through her as he bent even closer and delicately licked the smear of cream from her lip in an action that was so intimate that every bit of her trembled in reaction. Just for a second her eyes met his, vulnerable, unguarded, then a familiar voice spoke and she jerked her head away from his light hold.

'Sorry, I didn't mean to interrupt you, but Daddy was wondering if he could have a word with you, Wyatt.'

'Of course.' He turned to smile at Carling, then looked back at Louise with a smile that made her heart roll over. 'You don't mind, do you, darling? I promise I won't be long.'

Louise nodded, afraid to speak in case he could hear the shakiness of her voice. What would it be like to have him smile at her that way and really mean it? She had no idea, just the sudden strangest longing to find out that shocked her rigid. Why should she want that from Wyatt? Why?

'Enjoying yourself, Louise?' There was little warmth in Carling's voice now that Wyatt had left them. Louise bit back a sigh, pushing the disquieting thoughts to the back of her mind to deal with whatever was to come next.

'Of course. It's been a lovely party, Carling. You obviously have a natural gift for making these arrangements work. Have you never thought about doing this for a living?'

Carling laughed as she shuddered delicately. 'I think not. Daddy would have a fit if I decided to go to work. I'm in the fortunate position of not needing to do something so mundane and boring.'

Louise smiled coolly, refusing to react to the other woman's open condescension. 'Really? It's a pity, though, in some ways. I always think that having to earn a living is character-building.'

The smile faded from Carling's lips. 'Work is for poor people. The women in Wyatt's circle don't need to work.'

'Then perhaps that's the reason why he chose me, do you think? He might have grown bored with all those women you mention, might find their attitude rather shallow and meaningless.'

Carling moved closer, her eyes filled with dislike. 'Don't try getting too clever, Louise. It could be your downfall. Wyatt will come to his senses soon and realise that you don't fit in with his lifestyle.' She turned to glance around the room, then looked back at Louise with a mocking smile. 'Take a good look round you, Louise, a good, long look, because this might be the closest you ever come to the life Wyatt leads. Even now he must be wondering what he's doing with you when he could have his pick from the cream of society. He's no fool; he'll come to his senses and realise what he's going to lose out on. Now if you'll excuse me I'd better circulate. A few of us are planning on going to the casino later, but I'm sure you won't want to come,

Louise. I doubt if it's your idea of *worthy* entertainment.'

She turned to go, then stopped and glanced back with a malicious curl of her lips. 'By the way, I am glad that you've enjoyed tonight. I told you I wanted it to be special for you...something pleasant to remember when Wyatt comes to his senses at last.'

Louise watched her go, wishing there was some way she could have the satisfaction of watching her eat her words in the future, but that would never happen. After tomorrow she wouldn't see Wyatt again, and although he would probably leave a decent interval before announcing that their engagement was off it still wouldn't stop Carling from thinking she'd been proved right. It was the thought of how Carling would gloat that upset her, of course. It had nothing to do with the fact that after tomorrow she wouldn't feature in Wyatt's life at all.

The storm broke in the early hours of the morning. Louise lay in bed, listening to the rumbling of the thunder as lightning flashed against the window. The party had broken up around midnight, when most of the guests had left for the casino, but although she'd come straight up to her room she hadn't slept. Her mind was just too busy to allow her to relax enough to sleep.

Tossing the sheet aside, she got up and walked over to the window, resting her head against the coolness of the glass as she watched the storm unfolding. There was something elemental and awe-inspiring about the sheer volume of noise, the brilliance of the forks of lightning as they speared towards the earth. It was nature at its most magnificent, cruel and relentless, yet possessing a strange beauty that tugged at her emotions.

As the storm started to move away she sighed and turned to go back to bed, then realised that there was no point. She wouldn't sleep now any better than she'd done before, and suddenly the thought of lying there, going over and over everything that had happened, was more than she could bear.

Quickly she drew her robe from the end of the bed and slipped it on, then made her way from the room down to the library. Lawrence had an extensive collection of books, so surely she could find something to while away a few hours until the morning. Straight after breakfast she'd pack her things, then she'd be ready whenever Wyatt wanted to leave. Then that would be the end of this whole unhappy affair.

There was a strange heaviness in her heart as she pushed the library door open and switched on the small desk lamp. Deep down she knew she should be glad that it was nearly at an end and that soon she'd be able to put Wyatt and all the trouble he'd caused her behind her. But she was honest enough to admit that wasn't how she felt at all, and it bothered her.

'Did the storm wake you, or couldn't you sleep either?'

She dropped the book she was holding and swung round, her eyes widening as she suddenly spotted Wyatt sitting in one of the huge wing-back chairs. Despite the hour, he was still dressed, although he'd shed his jacket and rolled the sleeves of his shirt up, leaving his tanned forearms bare. For a long, tense moment he just studied her in silence, then picked up the heavy crystal glass that was sitting on a table beside the chair and raised it aloft with a mocking smile that cut into her heart. 'This is a night for toasts, isn't it, Louise? So let me make another one: to us and everything we've achieved here.'

Louise swallowed to ease the tightness in her throat, but her voice was husky. 'Does that mean that Lawrence has signed the contract?'

He tossed the drink back then refilled the glass, cradling it in his hand as he swirled the liquor round and round. 'Not yet, but it's all over bar that, everything worked out to the last letter. A couple more days and the hotels will be mine. So here's to us, Louise.' He took another long swallow of the whiskey, then set the glass down with a thud that made her jump. Louise studied him in confusion. He'd told her himself he'd waited for years to finalise this deal, yet there'd been no trace of the elation he should surely feel in his voice.

'There's nothing wrong, is there? You don't foresee any problems?' she asked softly, watching him.

He smiled faintly, his eyes returning to her face in a look that made her feel strangely uneasy. 'No. It's all gone like clockwork, thanks to you.'

She shrugged, bending to pick up the book and smooth its pages with hands that trembled slightly. 'I don't believe that I played a major role in this. From what I've learned about you, Wyatt, you would have got those hotels one way or another even without any help.'

'Perhaps, but let's just say that you have made things flow that bit smoother. So another toast, to the best little actress I've ever had the good fortune to meet. May every role you play in the future be equally successful.' He downed the rest of the whiskey and Louise wondered why she felt the most ridiculous urge to cry. If he'd meant that as a compliment, then it fell far short of being that.

She turned to slide the book back into place on the shelf, feeling sadness welling inside her. Wyatt would always consider her to be nothing but a cheat and a liar, a woman who would do anything for money, and suddenly she knew she had to tell him the truth.

She turned back, her face very pale but filled with determination as she met his sardonic gaze. 'There's something I want to tell you, and I want you to promise that you'll listen. You owe me that much.'

'Tell me what? If this is confession time, honey, then save your breath. I know all I need to know about you. The same goes for if you've suddenly come up with some new fanciful tale about what you *really* do with your life.'

'There's nothing fanciful about it! It's going to be the truth, every word of it. Not that I expect you to believe me; you're too pigheaded for that. But at least I'll have the satisfaction of knowing that I tried to make you understand how wrong about me you are!'

'I doubt if you even know what the truth is after all the lies you must have told.' He stood up and came towards her, strangely intimidating in the dim lamp-light with his face set and his pale eyes glittering. Louise felt her heart sink, but she stood her ground. They only had a few hours left, and somehow she was going to make him listen to what she had to say!

'And you do, eh? Come on, Wyatt, even you can't be so arrogant as to believe that you *never* make a mistake?'

His eyes narrowed at her biting sarcasm, but he merely smiled. 'I make as many mistakes as the next guy, but I haven't made any about you, sweetheart. I know who you are and what you are, and there's nothing else I need to know. And there is definitely nothing that you can dream up to convince me otherwise.'

'Not even if I back it up with indisputable evidence? Surely then you'd have to admit that you just might be wrong?'

He laughed deeply. 'What kind of evidence? Testimony from one of your gentleman friends? Oh, I don't doubt that you can get one of them to swear you're purer than the driven snow. Women like you can cast a spell over a man, Louise, make him want to believe anything you care to tell him, but you and I both know the truth. The funny thing is that it doesn't stop me from wanting you.'

Suddenly, in the space of a single heartbeat, the atmosphere shifted, a throbbing tension humming in the air between them. Louise took a tiny shallow breath, almost afraid to move in case she triggered a reaction she wasn't sure she could handle. She licked her parched lips, then felt the blood thunder to her head as she saw the way his eyes centred on the action in a look she could feel deep inside.

'Wyatt, I——'

He pressed his thumb against her mouth, stroking it around the moist softness, his eyes glittering fiercely into hers as he took a step towards her so that she could feel the heat of his body flowing over her skin. 'Don't. No more lies, no more pretence. I know what you are, but it means less than nothing to me compared with this ache I feel to have you.' He drew his thumb from her mouth and slid it down the column of her neck to let it rest against the pulse that was beating frantically at its base. 'This is the only kind of truth I need. I want you and you want me.'

He caught the lapels of her robe, crushing the soft fabric as he drew her closer and held her there. 'You've lived your whole life as a lie up to now, so why not be truthful for once and admit what you really feel?'

'You're wrong!' There was a raw ache in her voice, an ache that was spreading through her whole body. He was right, she did want him almost to the point of madness, but to admit it to him would leave her so vulnerable that she was afraid.

'No, I'm not. That's what scares you.' He smoothed the silky fabric across her shoulders, smiling faintly when he saw the shock in her eyes at his correct assessment of the situation. Louise dropped her eyes, staring down at the front of his white shirt as she tried to fight the debilitating mixture of fear and desire. Despite what he'd just said, she couldn't afford to forget what had happened between them before, all those veiled half-threats. Was this his way of making her pay for her temerity?

The thought steadied her just enough to allow her to look up and meet his eyes. 'What is this all about, Wyatt? Are you trying to get your own back, or is it a way to add a few fringe benefits to our deal?' She laughed coldly, forcing scorn in her voice when she carried on. 'Sorry, but if it's the latter then you're doomed to disappointment. That fee you're paying me only covers the role I've been playing. It doesn't run to any...extras!'

His eyes narrowed dangerously. 'You'll get your money, my sweet. Don't worry about that. This has nothing whatsoever to do with any previous... arrangements we made. I just thought you might appreciate the chance to tell the truth for once, rather than all those lies.'

'So you know how I feel, do you? You have this wonderful insight into how my mind works?'

'I don't know about your mind, but your body...' He laughed softly as he drew her to him and tilted her face up to his, holding it firmly when she tried to turn away. When he spoke again his voice had dropped to a smoky timbre that stirred her senses. 'I have a good idea what your body feels, Louise.'

'I...I...No! Stop this, Wyatt. I won't let you... you—— '

He bent and kissed her mouth, swiftly, fiercely, then drew back before she could make any attempt to rebuff the caress. 'Seduce you? Are you sure? It's what you want, what we've both wanted for days now. Why not be honest enough to admit it? At least then I'd know you're capable of something more than lies!'

There was a note of fierce anger in his voice now that startled her. She'd thought that he was doing

this as some kind of punishment, yet it seemed there
was more to it than that. Did it really matter to him
if she was honest now? Would it perhaps help convince him that if she could tell the truth once she
could do so again? The thought was so tantalising
that it made her hesitate when what she should have
done was push him away, and he took advantage
of that momentary lapse in a devastatingly effective way.

With a rough curse he took her mouth in a kiss
that drove all the breath from her body and all
thoughts from her head. It was fire and ice, punishment and pleasure, so soul-stirring that she
whimpered. He seemed to be drawing the very es-
sence out of her as his lips drew a response she was
helpless to refuse. There was nothing left any longer
apart from her and Wyatt and this kiss that seemed
to spread into eternity.

When he drew back and stared into her shocked
eyes she was shaking, every bit of her trembling
with a fine, tight tension that she knew he felt. He
ran his hands lightly down her arms, then let them
slide around her as he drew her to him so closely
that she could feel the unmistakable evidence that
he was just as aroused as she.

'I want you, Louise.' He ground the words out,
his hands tightening for a moment before he eased
her away and stared down at her, waiting...
waiting...

'I...I want you too.' It was no more than a
whisper, her voice breaking on a confession that
was wrung from her. Deep down, a tiny voice was
warning her that she was making a mistake, but she
cut it off. It might be madness, the biggest mistake

of her life, but she was going to make it anyway. Wyatt had wanted truth from her, and this was the only kind of truth she could give him that he would believe.

She looked back into his eyes and repeated it, so that there could be no mistake about what she'd said. 'I want you!'

He had her in his arms before the last word had barely left her lips, his arms hard as he swept her off the ground and started towards the door. He paused as he swung it open, his eyes glittering fiercely as they met hers. 'You won't regret this, honey. Out of this whole mess this will be the one good memory you'll have to take away with you. I can guarantee it!'

Louise felt tears burning behind her eyes, but she fought to control them as she placed her mouth against his and kissed him. She would regret it. She would probably regret it until her dying day, but she couldn't prevent what was about to happen. To have Wyatt love her and love him back was the only act of honesty in a relationship that had been founded upon lies.

CHAPTER NINE

LOUISE and Wyatt made love slowly, taking their time to learn the new, unfamiliar contours of each other's body. Wyatt seemed to know exactly how to touch her to make her tremble with need, but strangely she too seemed to know how to respond. She had never made love before with any man, never wanted this closeness and intimacy, yet she felt no fear, no embarrassment. She wanted this, wanted it with a desire that defied reason. It was a miracle that grew and grew with each slow, delicate touch, each softly lingering kiss, and filled her with a heady kind of joy.

When he captured her hands and held them away from him as he stared down into her face she smiled, her body arching up to press against his in a way that tore a groan from his lips. 'God, Louise! Have you any idea what you're doing to me? I'm as het up as a boy with his first woman!'

'Good.' The soft word whispered from her just a moment before she slid her mouth along the strong column of his neck, the tip of her tongue tracing his skin in tiny fleeting touches that sent a deep shudder rippling through him. He captured her chin and turned her head so that he could take her mouth in a hungry kiss that made her whole body throb with need, an echo of what she'd felt in him. Slowly he drew his mouth from hers and let his lips trail down her throat, then carry on to the rigid tip of her breast. Delicately he caressed it with his tongue, then drew it further into his mouth and bit gently. Louise whimpered, her body arching, taut as a bow, her hands clenching and unclenching on the pillow beside her head. When he turned his attention to her other breast and repeated the slow, tormenting actions she cried out, naked desire echoing in her voice.

He raised his head, his face faintly flushed, the tanned skin stretched tight over the lean planes as he studied her passion-drugged eyes. 'This is the truth, isn't it? For once in your life there's no pretence. What you're feeling now is real!'

There was a kind of triumph in his deep voice that grated.

'Wyatt, I——'

She got no further, all thoughts fleeing as he captured her mouth again in a kiss of burning passion that sent the blood thundering in dizzying waves through her veins. When his leg slid between hers she made no move to stop what was about to happen. This was meant, right from the moment they had met, and all she wanted was the fulfilment that she sensed he could give her.

Her hands slid up his back, her nails biting into the smooth, sweat-slicked skin as she drew him to her and held him, feeling the thundering beat of his heart against her breast, an echo of the heavy beating of her own. She wanted this, wanted it so much because she loved him.

The thought came from nowhere, sliding quietly into her mind. She felt no shock, just a sudden relief that so many unanswerable questions had now been answered so simply. She loved Wyatt; that was why she had always responded to him, why she was responding to him now. Her mind had kept as a secret something her body had always known.

A fierce joy consumed her and she arched towards him as he drove deep into her softness, then gasped with pain as her body resisted. He stilled at once, quivering with shock as realisation hit him.

'Damn you, Louise! Damn you to hell!'

There was a moment when she thought that he was going to draw back, then he groaned deeply in something akin to anguish as passion claimed him as its victim and his body responded to the need he felt. He drove them both on, taking that first fleeting pain she'd felt and turned it into an ecstasy that had her calling his name over and over as they climbed to the heights and fell, spinning, back to earth.

Moonlight filtered through the window, bathing the room in its silvery pale light. It seemed to steal all the colour from the rich furnishings, turning the whole room into a negative of light and dark, shade and shadow. Louise sat on the edge of the bed, huddled into her robe, wondering why she felt as though she was a part of the strange scene. She felt somehow unreal, devoid of light and colour, as though the moonlight had touched her and stolen all the warmth and life from her body.

'Why, Louise? What did you hope to gain from what you did? Tell me, damn you!'

The voice came from the door, but she didn't turn. She didn't need to. She'd known he would come back ever since he'd left. There had been something in his pale eyes that had told her the torment hadn't ended when he'd pulled away from her and dressed before walking from her room. She'd got up from the rumpled bed and showered and dressed in her robe, then sat down again to wait for him, wondering what she would say to the questions. But he was here now and she still didn't have any answers, or at least none that she would give him. The love she'd so recently discovered was too precious to reveal and listen to him try to destroy it with harsh words. When she left here it would be all she had to take with her to see her through the long, lonely days to come.

'I can't tell you why, Wyatt,' she said, softly, staring at the window.

'Can't or won't?' He closed the door with a restrained violence that was far more terrifying than any show of anger. When he stopped in front of her Louise forced herself to look up at him, then looked away, feeling her heart tearing itself into a thousand tiny pieces. He hated her, now more than ever, hated her for what he'd seen as yet more trickery and deception.

'I still can't believe what happened, can't believe that you...you...' It was the first time that she'd ever heard that note of uncertainty in his voice, and she smiled bitterly.

'That I am—or rather, was—a virgin. Is that what you are trying to say, Wyatt?'

'Yes! It just doesn't fit with what I know about you. How could it be so?'

'When I lead the kind of life I do?' She laughed with a touch of hysteria, then bit her lip, knowing she was within an inch of losing control. 'Does it

make you wonder if you just might be wrong about
me, Wyatt?'

He shook his head, his pale eyes glittering cold
as ice as they met hers. 'I'm not wrong! This is just
another twist to an old tale.' He ran a hand through
his hair, then laughed harshly. 'I'd say that you are
far more clever than I gave you credit for, honey.
What have you been holding out for for so long—
some poor fool who's rich enough to pay for the
privilege of knowing he's the first? Well, if you were
hoping that I'd feel especially grateful, my sweet,
I'm afraid you're doomed to disappointment!'

His cruelty hurt so much that she wondered how
she could bear it. She wanted to plead with him to
understand, beg him to listen to what she wanted
to tell him, but what would be the point in doing
that? He would never change his mind about her
even though he had proof that he'd been wrong all
along.

It was pride that held her together, pride that
brought her to her feet to face him. 'There's none
so blind as those who refuse to see; isn't that a fact,
Wyatt? But I don't intend to waste my breath trying
to convince you just how wrong you are.' She
glanced at the small clock on the bedside table, then
stared quietly back at him. 'It's very late. I'm tired,
so I'd be glad if you would leave now. I really don't
think that there is anything left to say.'

He swore roughly as he caught her arm and
dragged her to him, holding her just a hair's breadth
away from his powerful body. He'd not bothered
to put his shirt back on, dressing only in the black
trousers, his broad chest bare. Louise could feel the
heat of his bare skin, smell the musky aroma of his

body, and a pain so sharp and intense that it nearly tore her in two cut through her.

'Wyatt, I——'

He cut her off, his eyes like steel, his fingers biting into the soft flesh he'd caressed such a short time before. 'Did you really think I'd fall for such a trick? That I'd be willing to pay—and pay heavily— for sleeping with you?'

'It wasn't like that. You . . . you were the one who started it by making me admit how I felt!'

If he heard the pain in her voice he made no concession for it. He smiled harshly down at her, his eyes filled with contempt. 'Yes, I did. At least I can feel satisfaction at being proved right, but as for the rest of it . . . that priceless gift you decided to give me . . . Sorry, honey, but you should have saved it for someone who would really appreciate it. It doesn't alter our agreement one iota, understand?'

She pushed him away, her whole body shaking with a tension she could barely control. 'I understand. Don't worry, Wyatt. I don't intend to make a scene. After all, you can't blame a girl for trying, can you?'

Just for a moment she thought that he was going to strike her as his face turned into a mask of rage. Then he turned and strode to the door and left without a word. Louise sank down on the bed, clasping her hands so tightly that her fingers ached. She wouldn't break down. Not yet. Not in this house. Not in front of Wyatt. Pride was all she had left.

* * *

Miami lay white and gleaming under the July sun.
Louise picked up her bag and followed Wyatt to
the car that was waiting to collect them at the
airport. He'd barely said a word on the flight back,
and Louise hadn't tried to make conversation.
They'd said everything that needed to be said.

Her heart was heavy as she handed the driver her
bag and slid into the back of the black limousine.
It felt like a lifetime since she'd arrived at this very
airport, buoyed up with excitement about the
holiday. Now she felt years older and infinitely
weary. All she wanted was to go home and put this
all behind her, but it was never going to be as simple
as that.

'Where do you want me to drop you? The hotel?'
Apart from a few carefully impersonal sentences
over breakfast as he'd carried on the pretence for
the benefit of Carling and Lawrence, it was the most
he'd said to her all morning. Louise glanced at him
as he closed the car door, then turned back to stare
out of the window with a brief nod of agreement.

'Will they have kept the room for you? Miami
is busy at this time of the year.'

As if he cared one way or the other what happened to her! There was an edge to her voice as she
answered, 'The room is booked and paid for until
tomorrow. There shouldn't be any problem, so
don't worry, Wyatt, I won't come running to you
for help. Once you've dropped me off, then we can
part company.'

His jaw tensed at the open sarcasm, but he merely
smiled. 'After we've finalised our business
arrangements, Louise.'

She glared back at him, hating him and loving him at the same time. 'Don't worry, I haven't forgotten about that. How could I when it's the one thing that's made this whole unpleasant incident worth while?' She shuddered delicately, looking straight into his eyes, although it almost broke her heart to lie to him. 'Ten thousand dollars should go a long way towards making up for having to be with you.'

His eyes glittered back into hers. 'I'd be careful what I said if I were you. You don't have the cash in your hands yet. It would be a simple enough matter to decide to break our agreement.'

'And run the risk of my telling Lawrence what has been going on? I can just imagine dear Carling's anger if she found out the truth, can't you? And you did say that the contract isn't signed, yet, I believe.'

'Don't even think about it!' His voice dropped, rough and dangerous now, as he leant across the seat and hauled her to him. 'I don't like threats, Louise.'

'Yet you are more than happy to use them to your own ends? What a hypocrite you are, Wyatt. I'll be glad to see the back of you all right!'

'I'm sure you will, but it won't be just yet.' He tossed her hand away as he glanced at his watch. 'I'm due to meet with Lawrence's lawyers in a couple of hours' time. Once I have confirmed that the contract is ready, then I'll pay you, not before. Just a precaution, you understand.'

'Do what you like. I don't give a damn!' Tears were clouding her vision, but she held them back.

He was determined to treat her with contempt to
the bitter end, it seemed.

When the car glided to a halt in front of the hotel
she jumped out before he could offer to help her.
She stood stiffly while the driver lifted her case from
the boot, refusing his offer to carry it inside for
her. The car moved away and she stood and
watched it until it disappeared into the flow of
traffic, wondering where she would find the strength
from when Wyatt finally went out of her life for
good.

'Are you sure you won't come, Louise? I hate
leaving you here like this. You look . . . well, "lost"
is the only word that springs to mind.'

Carol sat down on the edge of the bed, studying
her with concern, and Louise tried her hardest to
reassure her.

'I'm fine. Honestly. Just a bit tired after that
party and the storm. Give me a couple of hours
and I'll be my old self.'

'Mmm, I wonder.' Carol glared almost fiercely
at her. 'Look, I'm probably completely out of order
saying this, but are you sure that nothing happened
between you and that guy, Lord? Simon and I have
been asking around, and he has quite a reputation,
I can tell you. He plays the field all right.' She held
her hands up. 'OK, OK, I know it's none of my
business, but I was worried about you. You took
off with him before we'd had chance to really talk
things through and make you see how dangerous
it could be. You knew nothing at all about him,
Louise. For all you knew, he might have been a

white-slave trader rather than one of the toughest businessmen in the USA!'

Louise smiled, used to Carol's love of the dramatic. Her friend might be one of the best staff nurses on the wards, but she did have a penchant for being a shade over-imaginative. 'Well, he isn't, or, if he does it as a sideline, obviously he didn't think that I'd fetch much on the open market. I'm back, aren't I? What more can I say?'

'A great deal, from the look of you! There's more to this than you're admitting to, Louise Carter. I just wish I had more time to prise the details out of you, but I have to go, if you're sure you'll be all right. Simon would love to have you join us, I know he would. It is our last night here, after all.'

'And I have no intention of spoiling it for you both by playing gooseberry. Go and enjoy yourself, Carol. I'll be fine, honestly.'

'Well, if you're sure...' Carol stood up, smiling mischievously. 'I know you only agreed to go with Lord to teach him a lesson, but are you sure he didn't teach you a thing or two? Make sure that when we leave tomorrow you won't be leaving your heart behind. If you feel anything for him, then for heaven's sake forget your pride and tell him... before it's too late!'

Carol left and Louise got up from the bed, wrapping her arms tightly around herself to ward off the sudden chill. If only she could take her friend's advice and tell Wyatt how she felt! But what was the point in even thinking about that when she knew that all he would do was laugh in her face? She couldn't bear to have that happen, couldn't bear the thought of him accusing her of making up

more lies, couldn't bear the thought of seeing him
again!

She glanced round the room, her eyes dropping
to the suitcase standing at the end of the bed. She'd
not bothered to unpack, contenting herself with
taking out her robe and a few toiletries, and now
she wondered if all along she had known what she
must do, that she must leave before Wyatt came
back to end this strange relationship for good.

It took only minutes to dress in a plain white
pleated skirt and T-shirt, and a few seconds more
to re-pack her robe and clear the bathroom. Once
she was ready Louise took a last look round the
elegant bedroom, then picked up the case, checking
that she had the note she'd written for Carol to tell
her what she was doing. She would leave it at the
reception desk for her friend, a brief explanation
that she'd gone to the airport to try to book on to
an earlier flight home. Undoubtedly Carol would
be full of questions when they met up again, but
she would worry about how to answer them later.
For now all she could concentrate on was leaving
before Wyatt came to find her, and broke what was
left intact of her heart.

What had started out as a dream come true—
winning the luxury holiday—had ended up as a
nightmare that was going to haunt her for the rest
of her life.

There was no one on the reception desk when she
arrived downstairs. Setting her bag down, she rang
the bell, then stood tapping her foot impatiently as
she waited for someone to answer. Outside a coach
had just drawn up, bringing a group of holiday-
makers back from one of the organised trips around

the city. Louise shot a glance at the closed door to
the office, then moved aside to avoid them as they
spilled into the hotel's foyer.

'So there you are. Is this just a fortunate coincidence finding you down here, or were you
waiting for me . . . eager to get your hands on the
money?'

Her blood ran cold as she heard the familiar voice
behind her. She swung round, her heart pounding
so fast that she felt breathless. 'I . . . I . . . of course.'
She forced a smile, watching the way his eyes narrowed, cold and pale as they searched her face. 'A
coincidence, I mean. I had no doubt that you'd be
here to pay me what you owe. There's too much at
stake to take any chances now, isn't there, Wyatt?'

He swore softly as he caught her by the elbow
and half dragged her across the foyer and out
through the sliding doors that led on to the terrace.
'You never learn, do you, Louise? You always have
to push things just that bit too far!'

'Me push you? I didn't know I was even capable
of that. That *does* surprise me, darling.' One part
of her couldn't quite believe what she was saying,
couldn't understand where she was finding the
strength from when what she really wanted to do
was fall in a heap at his feet and beg him to let her
explain. But somehow she managed to find it,
enough to stop her from breaking down.

'Let's cut the acting, shall we? From here on in
our relationship is at an end. So save all your en-
dearments for those who appreciate them.' He
smiled harshly, glancing back at the busy foyer
before looking back at her with a question in his
eyes. 'Perhaps you weren't waiting for me after all,

Louise. As you said, you knew that money was
more or less in the bank, so maybe you'd already
set your sights on your next...project.' He laughed
slowly, the sound more insulting than she could ever
have imagined it could be. 'I recognised one of the
men who was getting off that coach as I came in.
The same man who was singing your praises to me
by the pool that day. I must say that I admire your
single-mindedness, honey. You don't believe in
letting the grass grow under your feet, do you? Not
when you have a living to earn.'

How could he? After what had happened between them last night, how could he just stand there
and say such things? For a moment Louise just
stood and stared at him, every bit of pain and hurt
she felt shining in her tear-misted eyes, then turned
and headed back inside.

'Wait! Don't you walk out on me!' He caught
her by the shoulder, a restrained violence in the
action as he swung her around and glared down
into her face. 'This isn't finished yet, not by a long
way.'

'Isn't it? Why, what else is there to say, Wyatt?
Have you more insults you want to make, more accusations? I'd have thought you'd said all there was
to be said along those lines, but, if it pleases you
to carry on, then do so.' Her voice was flat, devoid
of feeling now. She was hurting so much that she
doubted if anything he said could hurt her any
more, but she should have known that he'd find a
way to torment her.

His hands tightened on her shoulders, his eyes
blazing as he hauled her to him and held her so

close that she could barely breathe. 'Damn you! Damn you to hell, Louise, for everything!'

There was a moment when her mind had a chance to wonder at the bitterness in his voice, and then he bent and kissed her with a bruising, insulting force that made her struggle wildly. Then just as suddenly he shoved her away from him, his eyes cutting into hers for one long moment before he slid his hand into his jacket pocket and pulled out a long white envelope. He tossed it at her, his mouth curled in derision when she made no attempt to catch it. 'Careful, sweet. You don't want to lose that, do you? Not when you've worked so damned hard to earn that fee.' He turned to walk away, then stopped and glanced back. 'Oh, by the way, I added a bonus to the total, a little something extra for last night, you understand?'

He pushed the doors apart and walked back into the hotel without another word. Louise stared after him, unaware of the tears falling slowly down her ashen face. Slowly she bent and picked up the envelope, smoothing the crumpled paper out between her shaking fingers before ripping it open and pulling out the cheque it contained. The words blurred in front of her eyes and she blinked hard, then stared down at the thin sheet of paper, every bit of her aching at what it represented. Such a lot of money, yet no amount of money in the world was enough to pay for a broken heart and a love that was lost forever.

But Wyatt would never, ever know that now, and that was the most painful part of it all.

CHAPTER TEN

'So JUST keep an eye on Mr Jones in the end bed. He's been a bit restless during the night. I don't think there's any need for concern, but a bit of extra attention wouldn't come amiss.' Louise handed the file of notes over to Carol and smiled wearily. 'And that's it. It's all yours, my friend. I'm going home to a well-earned sleep.'

Carol grinned, but her eyes were concerned as they studied the waxen pallor of her friend's face. 'Well, make sure that *is* what you do. I know night shift is a drag, but you look worse than I've ever seen you looking.'

'Nice to know you can rely on your friends for comfort.' Louise smiled to take the sting out of her words. 'Don't worry, mother hen. I shall be a good girl and go straight home to bed as promised.' But would she sleep? The question ran through her brain as she gave Carol a final wave and collected her cape and bag. That was the real trouble, of course. It didn't have anything to do with a week of working nights. No matter how hard she tried, she just couldn't seem to sleep. Her body ached with weariness, her mind begged for the release of sleep, but every time her head hit the pillow she came wide awake. When would it ever end? When would she start to put what had happened in America behind her and live again?

170

There was no answer to the question now, just as there hadn't been one for the past month since she'd got back. It wasn't only Carol who was starting to query why she looked so drained either. Only the previous day her mother had called round at her flat and delicately tried to find out what was troubling her, but Louise hadn't been able to talk to her about it. The hurt was just too raw and ran too deep to talk about even with her mother, whom she loved dearly. It was something she was going to have to learn to come to terms with, because there was no cure for what she felt. She still loved Wyatt, loved him with her heart, her soul, with every crazy bit of herself, and that was just the way it was going to be.

The sun was shining when she pulled up in front of the tall Victorian building where she rented her flat. Louise parked her car, then climbed out and stretched as she drew in a lungful of the warm, sweet air. Although the house was minutes from the heart of the city, it was quiet here, overlooking the green stretch of grass that marked the beginning of Sefton Park. She glanced up at the window of her flat, then back across the park, feeling strangely loath to go inside and shut herself in her room to make another abortive attempt at sleep.

Tossing her cap and cape into the back of the car, she locked the door then walked slowly on to the grass and slipped off her shoes, dangling them from her fingers as she carried on walking. The grass was cool and slightly damp against her stock-inged feet, reminding her vividly of the time she'd

walked barefoot along the beach on the night of
the engagement party.

'Wyatt!' She whispered his name softly, lovingly,
allowing herself the rare freedom of saying it aloud.
She'd tried so hard to blank out all the memories
in these past lonely weeks, but maybe that had been
a mistake. Maybe she should have allowed herself
to think about everything that had happened.
Maybe she should do that, face the pain and hurt
and futility of what she felt and in that way find
release from it.

She walked over to a clump of trees and sat down
on the rough grass, letting her mind drop all the
barriers she'd tried so hard to erect, and slowly the
memories came back, one by one, so vivid and
painful that she cried out. She pressed a hand to
her lips to stop the sound, glancing round, afraid
that someone might have heard, but the park was
empty at this early hour of the morning, the peace
and quiet barely disturbed by the throb of an engine
as a car drew up not far from where she'd left hers
parked. Louise glanced incuriously at it, then closed
her eyes, letting her mind drift back to a time that
was both painful and beautiful, and felt a shudder
run through her as the memories came again, un-
curling inside her head: Wyatt holding her so
close—too close—as they'd danced that night at the
party, his pale eyes glittering with amusement; his
lips brushing her temple, warm and hard; his face
filled with desire as he'd loomed over her just an
instant before they'd become one...

'Wyatt!' Tears were coursing down her face now,
but she couldn't feel them, caught up in the agony
and the ecstasy as the final barrier crumbled.

'Don't! Sweet heaven, Louise...don't!'

The shock was so great that she felt her heart stop. For a moment that touched eternity she kept her eyes closed, terrified to open them. It was just her mind playing tricks, that was all. Some kind of crazy hallucination.

'Won't you look at me, honey? I know I don't deserve anything from you, but please!' His fingers were gentle as he caught her chin, so gentle that they might almost have been a part of that hallucination if her body hadn't instantly recognised as real the touch it craved so much. Her eyes flew open and she stared at him with a blatant, undisguised hunger. He swore roughly and knelt down beside her, his hand shaking as he cupped her cheek.

'I don't know what to say, Louise. Words aren't enough to make up for what I did...what I said to you!' There was a note of anguish in his deep voice that shocked her. She drew in a short, sharp breath, then let it out slowly as she stared into his pale, glittering eyes, seeing all the regret, all the pain...and something else, something that made her feel both giddy and afraid.

She scrambled to her feet, smoothing the skirt of her navy dress, her face very pale. 'Wh-why have you come here, Wyatt?' She glanced round, watching a woman leading a dog across the grass on the end of a long lead. The sound of its happy barking carried in the quiet air, yet it seemed as though it were happening a million miles away from where she was standing staring down at Wyatt. She forced her eyes back to him, watching as he stood up and pushed the dark hair back from his forehead in a gesture that was so achingly familiar that she could have wept. 'How did you find me?'

He smiled harshly, a strange bitterness in his voice. 'It isn't difficult to find anything out if you have the kind of connections I have. All it takes is the desire to do so and the information is there for the asking, every scrap of it.'

Her heart turned over at the way he said that. He sounded like a man in torment, a man who had suffered, but why? She took a half-step towards him, then hesitated, suddenly afraid. 'I don't understand,' she said quietly. 'Just what do you want with me now? I . . . I thought our agreement had come to an end in Miami.'

His face went rigid, every line so tight that he looked as though he'd been carved from stone. 'Yes, it did! The arrangement I forced you to agree to.' He turned and slammed his fist against the rough bark of the tree, seemingly unaware of the damage he inflicted on himself. 'I did a lot of things a month ago that I should never have done, Louise!'

'Your hand . . . Wyatt.' She rushed forwards and caught his bleeding hand between both of hers, staring up into his set face with concern. 'Look what you've done!'

He barely glanced at it. 'It doesn't matter. Nothing matters apart from the fact that you give me time to apologise for what I did to you.'

Her heart ached, but she forced a trembling smile, trying to hide the agony she felt. She didn't want apologies; they were merely a sop which wouldn't stop the pain. What she really wanted from him was something he could never give her. 'It doesn't matter now. Obviously you must have found out the truth about me, so there doesn't seem any point in discussing it further.'

'And you're not interested in *how* I found out the truth?' There was just the faintest trace of anger in his voice now that stung her into replying.

'Should I be? *I* knew what the truth was all along. It was you who were so stubborn, so all-fired sure that you were right about how I earned my living! Why should I want to listen to anything you have to say to me now, Wyatt Lord?' She picked up her shoes and slipped them on, then stared coldly at him, hating the way her eyes feasted traitorously on the muscular lines of his strong body. Although he was still deeply tanned there were new lines around his carved mouth, a hint of suffering she'd never noticed before. Just for a moment all the love she felt for him blossomed and filled her with all its warmth and wonder before ruthlessly she drove it from her mind. 'If you made this journey just to say that you were sorry, then I'm afraid you've had a wasted journey. I don't want your apologies. I don't want any damned thing you can give me to ease your conscience, thank you!'

She started past him, her breath coming in laboured spurts, her heart hammering fast and furious in her breast. One step, two… She'd almost reached the road before he spoke, his voice filled with an anger that far outstripped her own.

'I didn't come just to apologise, damn you, woman!'

She spun round, her face unconsciously haughty, her grey eyes stormy as she raised a mocking brow. 'Indeed? Then why did you come? Surely not to ask for your money back now that you realise I don't need it to keep me?' She laughed lightly. 'Sorry, Wyatt. You're too late for that. Your nice fat cheque has been cashed already!'

His anger was almost tangible as he strode towards her and stopped far too close. 'Has it indeed? You didn't waste much time in benefiting from what happened, did you, Louise? There I was imagining that you'd be distraught, but you were out spending the cash!'

Her hand caught his cheek a stinging blow. He had no time to side-step, just as she'd had no time to think twice before administering it. He deserved it, that and a whole lot more, for everything he'd done, all the pain and hurt he'd inflicted upon her and was still inflicting now! 'For your information, Lord, *I* haven't spent a penny of your rotten money. Understand? Not one penny! I don't need your money or anyone else's to support me. I earn what I need! Your cheque was paid in to the hospital's scanner appeal fund. I imagine you'll be receiving a letter of thanks very shortly from the trustees. They were most impressed that an American businessman cared enough to make such a generous donation. And it was generous, of course: ten thousand dollars for my part in tricking the Huttons, plus another five thousand for my virginity! At least I'll always have the satisfaction of knowing that my loss was a benefit to innumerable people!'

She turned to walk across the road, feeling the tears gathering in her eyes. She wanted to hate him so much, yet she couldn't. She loved him.

'Louise...please don't go like this.' His voice was deep and soft. It seemed to reach out and touch every part of her, filling her with so much pain that it brought her to a juddering halt next to her car. She reached out and laid her hand on the smooth, warm metal, feeling the solidness in a world that seemed to have nothing solid left in it as it tilted beneath her feet.

'Why? Why should I stay and listen to a word you have to say, Wyatt? Tell me that.' Her voice was just as quiet as his had been, yet it carried clearly to where he stood, echoing with all the hurt she felt, and she saw him flinch. For a moment he said nothing, his face betraying little of the inner battle she could sense he was fighting, then he smiled and took a slow, steady step towards her, holding her gaze all the time.

'Because I love you. I love you, Louise. I... love...you!' He shouted the words aloud, laughing as he saw the shock that darkened her eyes as he swept her into his arms and spun her round. He set her back down on the ground and linked his hands behind her waist, holding her as though she was the most precious burden he could ever hold. 'I love you, Louise. It's taken me one hell of a long time to face up to the fact, but I do!'

'I... I... I don't know what to say!'

'Of course you do. It's very simple, so just repeat it after me. I love you!' He tilted her face and stared into her eyes, smiling faintly as he bent and brushed a kiss across her parted lips. 'I know it's hard to take in, honey, but we both know it's the truth. Why else would you have slept with me that night on Paradise? You just aren't that sort of a girl.'

It was so wonderful finally to hear him say that that the tears started to run down her cheeks, and she sniffed. 'Now look what you've made me do.'

'I'm sorry. But you'll feel better if you admit how you feel. I did. I went through every kind of hell after you'd left. I couldn't understand what was wrong with me, then suddenly it hit me like a thunderbolt what it was. So come on, Nurse, administer the medicine and watch the patient start to recover.'

She smiled shakily at his gentle teasing, loving him more than ever. Was he telling her the truth? Did he love her? She searched his face and found the answer in the depths of his eyes, an answer she'd never thought to see. Joy ran through her so hotly and sweetly that she wanted to shout the words aloud, but instead she said them softly, whispering them to him alone. 'I love you, Wyatt. I don't need to make myself admit the fact. I knew it a while ago, that night after the party...' She couldn't continue, colour tinting her pale cheeks as she saw his eyes darken in understanding.

'When we made love.' His voice was husky, raw with emotion, his body trembling as he drew her to him and held her close. 'I should have known. It was so special that night, too marvellous to have been merely sex.' He laughed softly, feathering a kiss that made her shiver with need up her cheek. 'I think I did know, if I'm honest, and it scared me witless. The last thing I wanted was to fall in love with you!'

Louise laughed, drawing back to press a swift, tantalisingly soft kiss to his mouth, enjoying the way his breath caught and his hands tightened so betrayingly around her. 'The great Wyatt Lord

being scared of anything? That is something I want
to hear more about, along with a lot of other things,
like what made you change your mind, et cetera.
But I think we had better go inside, don't you?'
She glanced down at her uniform and grimaced.
'Don't men pick their time to tell you how they
feel? We spent all those days in paradise, and here
we are now!'

Wyatt grinned, letting his hands slide away as he
stepped back and took a long, lingering look at her
that brought the colour surging to her face and
made her heart suddenly realise it could work at
triple time. 'From where I'm standing you look just
fine. More than fine, in fact, my love.'

Flustered by the obvious appreciation in his face,
Louise hurriedly unlocked her car and took out her
cape and bag, then led the way up the path to the
front door, hearing the steady sound of his footsteps as he followed her. There was still so much
for them to discuss, so many things to clear up
before they could talk about the future, but they
would work things out now they had their love to
give them strength to deal with all the pain. Wyatt
loved her! She could build her future upon that
single fact alone!

'I didn't mean this to happen, at least not right
away.' Wyatt smiled as he pressed a lingeringly
tender kiss to her mouth, then smoothed the
tumbled hair back from her flushed cheeks. He
sighed contentedly as he leant back against the
pillows and drew her tighter into his arms, cradling
her against his strong body with a tenderness that
made her eyes mist with tears.

'I love you so much, Wyatt.' She pressed her mouth to his chin, feeling the way his heart leapt in immediate response under her hand. Drunk with the effect she seemed to have on him, she trailed her fingers across the warm muscles and heard his breath catch. He caught her hand and lifted it to his mouth to kiss every fingertip, then pressed it flat against his skin and held it there so that it couldn't wander again.

'Much as I enjoy what you were doing, sweetheart, I think we should talk right now, don't you?'

Louise gave a little moue of protest and bit him delicately, her teeth catching the warm, smooth skin at the base of his throat. 'Anyone ever tell you you're a killjoy, Wyatt Lord?'

He laughed deeply, his voice husky with echoes of desire. 'Not in this context. I've never been this way with any other woman, Louise, never had to fight my feelings just so that I can act rationally. I've always been able to separate my brain and my body before!'

Louise smiled, basking in the warmth of the compliment. She rolled over and stretched languidly, letting her leg brush the length of his, aware of the very predictable statement his body made at the intimate contact. 'Nice to know that I've achieved something no other woman has.' She frowned suddenly. 'I don't like to think about you and other women, Wyatt. I . . . realised that on the island, when I saw Carling in your room that night. I didn't know that she was altering the alarm for you at the time. I just remember feeling furious that she should be in there with you!'

He rolled on to his side, propping his head on his hand as he studied the troubled lines of her face. 'There won't be any other women now, honey. You're all I want and all I need. I never wanted Carling, although I don't think you should think too badly of her. She was instrumental in making me face up to how I felt about you.'

'Carling was?'

He laughed at her obvious disbelief. 'Yes. Carling found that note you wrote the night of the engagement party.'

'What note?'

He ran a lazily seductive finger down her nose, then sighed as he forced himself to drop his hand away from her mouth. 'The one promising to try your hardest to convince everyone that we were in love. She brought it to my office just after you left and challenged me as to what it meant.' His face darkened, stern and forbidding for a moment, before he smiled wryly. 'She said a lot of other things as well, about how unsuited you were to my lifestyle and about the fact that you earned your living by nursing and had actually won the holiday to Miami.'

Louise gasped as she sat bolt upright, forgetful of the fact that she wasn't wearing anything until she saw the way Wyatt's eyes dropped to her breasts with a look of such hunger that she felt weak with desire. Hurriedly she drew the sheet over herself, knowing that they had to talk this through. 'How did she know all that about me? I never told her.'

He sighed reluctantly. 'It's nothing short of a crime to hide such a beautiful body, but . . . Carling has the money and resources to find out what she wants to know, much the same as I can. Evidently our performance wasn't quite as convincing as we thought. It aroused her suspicions enough to start her digging for information.'

'But even with what she found out it wasn't proof that there was something funny about our engagement. So what did you tell her, Wyatt?'

'Nothing for quite a few minutes! I was so shocked by what she told me that I'm afraid my brain seized up for the first time in my life. I just sat there like stone as she trotted out one fact after another about you, facts I should have found out myself.' He sighed roughly, the memory obviously still painful to him. 'It was only when she started to call you names that I woke up. I must have scared the life out of her, I imagine, but she deserved it. I wasn't sitting there and having her speaking about you that way!'

A glow of warmth radiated through her body, and Louise smiled. 'I'm glad. Carling was never friendly, but I never imagined that you would take my side against her.'

He cupped her cheek tenderly and kissed her smiling mouth. 'Any time. It didn't make sense at first, the anger I felt at hearing her say such things about you. It was only later that I suddenly realised that I was in love with you and that whatever she said affected me too.'

'She can't have been pleased, though.'

He shrugged dismissively. 'She wasn't. In fact if I'd been in any doubt as to her true colours I'd have realised the truth about her then. She stormed out of the office threatening all sorts, not least of which was that her father would never sign the contract to sell the hotels.'

'No? But Wyatt, surely you haven't lost them?' She sat up and stared at him in concern. 'They are so important to you.'

'Not half as important as you are.' He kissed her again, lingeringly, with a hunger that made her tremble. He drew back slowly, his eyes meeting hers and holding. 'Those damned hotels are what drove us apart!'

'But they are also what brought us together in the first place.' She smiled shakily, linking her fingers through his to draw his hand to her mouth and kiss it softly. 'I'd hate for you to lose them because of me, Wyatt.'

'I don't think that will happen in the end. Hutton is too much of a businessman to let a good deal slip through his fingers. Oh, don't get me wrong; he'll make sure I pay and heavily for what's happened, but in the end I think he'll sell.'

'I'm glad. Will you tell me just why it was so important that you bought them?' She smiled wryly. 'It might be crazy, but I've always felt that was the key to so many things . . . the way you treated me, all your suspicions.'

'You're too astute, Louise.' For a moment a bleakness stole across his face, but then he smiled again and drew her close, settling her comfortably in the curve of his arm. 'I told you that my father sold them some time ago. What I didn't tell you was that he sold a lot more of our holdings at that time. He stripped the company down to the bone, even sold the house we'd had for so many years on

Paradise Island. That nearly broke my mother's heart.'

'But why? He must have had a good reason for doing so.'

He laughed shortly, just the tiniest trace of bitterness in the sound that made her ache. Reaching up, she smoothed his cheek, feeling some of the tension easing from him at the loving touch.

'He thought he had a good reason. He'd fallen in love with another woman, you see, a woman far younger than he was, and to keep up with the demands she made on him he sold everything he could lay his hands on until there wasn't much left to sell apart from the house we had in Miami. Fortunately that was in my mother's name, so he couldn't get his hands on it, but I don't doubt he would have sold it if he could!' He broke off and drew a deep breath, then continued slowly, painfully, speaking of a time that Louise knew instinctively he'd told no one else about. 'He was obsessed with Olivia almost to the point of madness, and she kept on and on with her demands until she'd bled him dry. The shock was too much for my mother. She had a heart attack and died just a week or so after my father finally came to his senses and realised what he'd done, but by then it was too late.'

'How...how awful. It must have been a dreadful time for you, Wyatt.'

'It was. I was just seventeen, going on eighteen, but old enough to understand what was happening. I hated my father for what he'd done to us, for all the anguish he gave Mother, and hated the woman who had driven him to it. I swore there and then I would get it all back, and that's what I've spent the last fifteen years of my life doing. It was an ambition fuelled by hatred, Louise. I'm not proud to admit that, but I want you to understand why.'

'And that's really why you acted the way you did with me. You saw in me what you took to be all the signs of a woman who would take a man for every penny, but you were wrong, Wyatt. Very, very wrong. That man in the hotel, Mr——'

He kissed her hard, his eyes suddenly fierce. 'I don't need any explanations, Louise! I realised a couple of weeks ago that I was completely wrong about you. I think I had half started to suspect it even before Carling came to me, but I was afraid to face the truth and admit what a mistake I'd made.' He laughed softly, sliding down against the pillows, drawing her with him. 'For the first time in my life my brain refused to blank out all the messages my body was trying to tell it! I knew you were innocent of all the charges I'd levelled against you, but I was scared witless to admit it! That's why I've taken so long to come here and find you. I was an out and out coward, because I knew that once we met again then that would be it.'

'What?' She raised one slender brow, then let her fingers take a gentle little stroll across his chest, feeling the sudden increase in his heartbeat with a tiny smile. 'What exactly is "it", Mr Lord?'

'Mmm, respect. I like that, honey, like it very much indeed. I think a wife should show due respect at all times to her husband!'

'Why, you male chauvinist! How...? What did you say?' It came out more as a gasp than a question as it suddenly hit her exactly what he'd

said, and he smiled with lordly arrogance. 'That a
wife should show due respect.'

'Let's skip the respect bit,' she said quickly, her
heart in her eyes as she searched his handsome face.
'It's the other that I'm interested in.'

He pretended to consider what she meant, then
groaned when her nails grazed against his bare skin.
'Hey, careful. You don't want to do any permanent
damage, do you? I wouldn't want to be ill on our
honeymoon.'

Suddenly all the teasing laughter faded and he
stared at her with so much love in his eyes that she
felt her heart swell. 'I love you, Louise. I want you
to marry me; that is if you can ever forgive me for
what I did to you.'

'That depends.' She smiled a trifle shakily,
moving closer into his arms so that her body
brushed softly against his.

'On what?' There was a deep huskiness in his
voice now, a faint tremble in the strong limbs that
touched hers.

'If you promise to love me forever and then some
more.' She ran a hand lightly down his cheek, then
touched his mouth, letting her fingers linger against
the warmth. 'I love you, Wyatt. I shall always love
you, but I want you to be sure that what you feel
for me is real and that it will last. I . . . I don't think
I could bear to lose you again.'

He smiled suddenly, sweeping her closer, holding
her as though he would never let her go again. 'I
think I can manage to do that!' He kissed her hard
and lovingly, then smiled into her eyes. 'I shall love
you forever and ever and then some more. Is that
good enough for you?'

'Not bad for starters, but I think you might need to keep on saying it for... oh, maybe the next sixty years or so to be truly convincing. After all, my love, I want to be certain that you're not just playing at love, but that it's the real thing this time!'

His hand slid up her body, his fingers teasing the gentle curves to life. 'Does this feel like playing?'

Louise felt the glow of happiness start deep inside her then spread throughout her whole body. She reached up and pulled his head down to hers, her lips just brushing softly against his as she whispered, 'No. It feels to me like the real thing all right.'

'It is. I love you, Louise.'

'And I love you too,' she replied. And then there was no need for any more words.

MILLS & BOON

CHRISTMAS CRACKERS

A cracker of a gift pack full of
Mills & Boon goodies. You'll find...

Passion—in *A Savage Betrayal* by Lynne Graham

A beautiful baby—in *A Baby for Christmas* by Anne McAllister

A Yuletide wedding—in *Yuletide Bride* by Mary Lyons

A Christmas reunion—in *Christmas Angel* by Shannon Waverly

Special Christmas price of 4 books
for £5.99 (usual price £7.96)

Published: November 1995

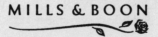

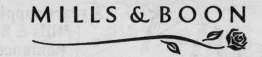

MILLS & BOON

Next Month's Romances

Each month you can choose from a wide variety of romance with Mills & Boon. Below are the new titles to look out for next month.

A WEDDING TO REMEMBER	Emma Darcy
A WOMAN OF PASSION	Anne Mather
FATE TAKES A HAND	Betty Neels
CALUM	Sally Wentworth
BEYOND REACH	Sandra Field
AN OBSESSIVE LOVE	Sarah Holland
THE SECRET BABY	Day Leclaire
NO HOLDING BACK	Kate Walker
MAKE-BELIEVE MARRIAGE	Renee Roszel
TOMORROW'S BRIDE	Alexandra Scott
BETWEEN MIST AND MIDNIGHT	Kathleen O'Brien
THE BLACK SHEEP	Susan Fox
PRISONER OF THE HEART	Liz Fielding
AN AMBITIOUS HEART	Marjorie Lewty
TO LOVE AND PROTECT	Kate Denton
THE MOON LADY'S LOVER	Vanessa Grant

Available from WH Smith, John Menzies, Forbuoys, Martins, Tesco, Asda, Safeway and other paperback stockists.

A years supply of Mills & Boon Romances — absolutely free!

Would you like to win a years supply of heartwarming and passionate romances? Well, you can and they're FREE! All you have to do is complete the wordsearch puzzle below and send it to us by 30th April 1996. The first 5 correct entries picked after that date will win a years supply of Mills & Boon Romance novels (six books every month — worth over £100). What could be easier?

STOCKHOLM	PARIS	HELSINKI	ANKARA
REYKJAVIK	LONDON	ROME	AMSTERDAM
COPENHAGEN	PRAGUE	VIENNA	OSLO
MADRID	ATHENS	LIMA	

N	O	L	S	O	P	A	R	I	S
E	Q	U	V	A	F	R	O	K	T
G	C	L	I	M	A	A	M	N	O
A	T	H	E	N	S	K	E	I	C
H	L	O	N	D	O	N	H	S	K
N	S	H	N	R	I	A	O	L	H
E	D	M	A	D	R	I	D	E	O
P	R	A	G	U	E	U	Y	H	L
O	A	M	S	T	E	R	D	A	M
C	R	E	Y	K	J	A	V	I	K

Please turn over for details on how to enter ➤

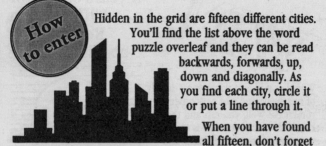

Hidden in the grid are fifteen different cities. You'll find the list above the word puzzle overleaf and they can be read backwards, forwards, up, down and diagonally. As you find each city, circle it or put a line through it.

When you have found all fifteen, don't forget to fill in your name and address in the space provided below and pop this page in an envelope (you don't need a stamp) and post it today. Hurry – competition ends 30th April 1996.

Mills & Boon Capital Wordsearch
FREEPOST
Croydon
Surrey
CR9 3WZ

Are you a Reader Service Subscriber?   Yes ❑   No ❑

Ms/Mrs/Miss/Mr _____

Address _____

_____

_____ Postcode _____

One application per household.

You may be mailed with other offers from other reputable companies as a result of this application. If you would prefer not to receive such offers, please tick box.   ❑

COMP495
D